INTONATION FOR STRINGS, WINDS, AND SINGERS

A SIX-MONTH COURSE

THEODOR PODNOS

THE SCARECROW PRESS, INC.
METUCHEN, N.J., AND LONDON   1981

Library of Congress Cataloging in Publication Data

Podnos, Theodor H.
    Intonation for strings, winds, and singers.

    Includes index.
    1. Musical temperament. 2. Tuning.
I. Title.
ML3809.P73   781'.22   81-9226
ISBN 0-8108-1465-X   AACR2

To my teacher Richard Burgin (1892-1981), who was associated with the Boston Symphony Orchestra for almost half a century:

Concertmaster,   1920-1966
Assistant conductor, 1935-1943
Associate conductor, 1943-1966

I am deeply indebted to him for the principles he taught me, some of which are contained in Chapter 19 of this book.

CONTENTS

---

v

INTONATION

FOR

STRINGS, WINDS, AND SINGERS

False intonation is a major impediment for aspiring artists.

"The individual tone is not music until it is directly connected with other tones, and tonal relations are not operative until tones and tonal combinations are in motion."
                                        --Paul Hindemith

INTRODUCTION

Why do listeners hear false tunings more readily than the player? While practicing, most violinists attempt to solve intonation problems by listening critically to the sounds they emit. Yet, when they perform, audiences still sometimes comment, "Out of tune." Evidently, hours of practice did not solve the intonation problems.

This book discusses four intonation systems. The first, by Tartini, has several disadvantages. The second and third derive from Campagnoli's writings and have helped musicians to a limited extent. The fourth system, while endorsing Campagnoli, explores intonation further and offers solutions for most tuning problems. This system is called Chordal Intonation.

Chordal Intonation is designed primarily for string instrumentalists but can be utilized also by singers and wind players. In this system, violinists learn in advance where to place their fingers, and wind players and singers where to poise notes by humoring.

Heifetz's teacher, Leopold Auer, also believed that intonations should be planned mentally before placing the fingers on the fingerboard (see page 9).

A study of recordings of great string artists reveals that intonation in accelerated speeds varies considerably from that in slower speeds. Within a diatonic octave, these artists used approximately twenty-four tunings in slow tempos and an extra sixteen in moderate and fast tempos. Also evident was the use of either major thirds of piano tunings, slightly sharpened major thirds, or those extremely sharpened.

It is well known that major scales should be played with raised thirds and sevenths, but in this volume these and many other alterations are systematized. In addition, much new material is presented.

Special discussions concern small- and large-sized semitones, enharmonicism, tonality, and intonation in running passages. Also treated are atonality, playing in ensembles, and playing with piano accompaniment.

Important facts have been duplicated in several instances, sometimes for emphasis and sometimes for readers who limit their attention to particular parts of a book.

Some readers may wish to proceed from page 1 to the end, or they may prefer to study "The Interval System" and "The Accidental System," then jump to the beginning chapters of "Chordal Intonation," returning to "Episode" for scientific explanations and laboratory tests of artists.

Teachers of beginners will find dispersed throughout the volume ninety exercises and etudes written in the first position. For intermediate or advanced students, there is material graded to every level, including a final chapter that describes "tricks of the trade." These students will gain more if they know harmony. The studies of double-stopping and seven string quartets provide solutions for soloists, ensemble players, and conductors.

Some voices, winds, and lower string instruments have a limited range. Thus, of a hundred and sixty exercises and etudes, a hundred and ten are written within a two-octave span.

To indicate the type of intonation recommended, four different arrows are used. Plain arrows ($\uparrow$ $\downarrow$) indicate much variation from piano tunings, whereas cut arrows ($\updownarrow$ $\updownarrow$) indicate slight alteration. Wind players may decide either to humor notes or use chosen fingerings. As for the questions "How much sharper, how much flatter?," both are answered mathematically in Chapters 4 and 5.

Because of the different problems existing among singers, winds, and strings, the book has been divided into sections. Violinists should read everything. Singers and wind players may omit particular sections, as indicated after many chapter headings.

In addition to handwritten music, photocopies of previously published works are provided in the interest of accuracy and the best interests of readers. Note that Ex. is the abbreviation for example, while Exer. is the abbreviation for exercise.

There are many reasons why one should acquire perfect intonation. In our Western culture, competition is keen. All ambitious musicians desire to play faster, cleaner, with a crisper staccato, more flowing legato, and a more beautiful vibrato and tonal quality than their fellow musicians. Each of these techniques requires separate study. Thus, musicians should also make a special study of intonation.

By applying Chordal Intonation, anxieties caused by intonation problems will be reduced considerably. In ensembles, arguments with fellow musicians concerning intonation will also be reduced. The principles of Chordal Intonation gradually become second nature, an asset retained for a lifetime. Constant intonation practice will be eliminated, and intonation will become a lesser problem.

To sum up, study of this book should result in less uncertainty for players, less impatience by conductors, shorter orchestra rehearsals, and, most important, less wasting of precious hours.

ACKNOWLEDGMENTS

I am deeply grateful to Allan Angoff, Harold Barlow, Martin Bookspan, Frank C. Campbell, Paul Clement, Brenda Cooper, Robert De Celle, Nathan Goldstein, Paul Heubert, Genevieve Kazdin, Fritz Kuttner, Arno Liberles, Ellen Liberles, Thad Marciniak, Marvin Mausner, David Randolph, Gustave Reese, Bernard Robbins, Louis Robbins, Boris Schwarz, Leon Thompson, Carolynn Weiner, Robert Weinrebe, and Oscar Weizner for suggestions, guidance, and assistance in translations, editing, recording, technical analysis, and research.

To Suzanne Bloch I extend a hearty thanks for reading the text in its early stages and offering much help regarding organization and graded levels of music education.

Professor Israel J. Katz had the kindness to read and edit much of the book. He gave the benefit of his knowledge concerning musicology and scholarly details.

Particular thanks go to Hugh Ross, conductor of the New York Schola Cantorum, who made valuable suggestions regarding the original manuscript and scrutinized the final writing. His fifteen years of encouragement spurred my work.

David Weiner will always be remembered for his meticulous music copying.

For permissions to use diagrams, photographs, quotes, musical scores, and other copyrighted material, grateful acknowledgment is made to various authors, publishers, collectors, libraries, and universities; complete citations have been stated in many cases.

I am also indebted to my wife, Elizabeth Podnos, who edited endlessly and had great patience in this time-consuming project.

ABBREVIATIONS

Acdtl.	Accidental System	min.	minor
aug.	augmented	n	
ca.	[circa] in approximately	c t	non chord tone
Chdl.	Chordal Intonation	op.	
c t.	chord tone	str. c's.	open string case
D. C.	[da capo] from the beginning	p.	page
dim.	diminished	perf.	perfect
D. S.	[dal segno] from the sign	pos.	position
enh. enhar.	enharmonic enharmonic	pp.	pages
Ex.	Example	Pyth.	Pythagorean Intonation
Exer.	Exercise	s.	semitone
fl.	flourished	T.	Tone (whole-tone)
Fr.	French	Vln.	Violin
Ger.	German	Vol.	Volume
harm.	harmonic	vps.	vibrations per second
Ibid.	[Ibidem] in that very place; (the same book as the last quoted)	⬆	slightly sharper
		↑	much sharper
Int.	Interval System	⬇	slightly flatter
M.	major	↓	much flatter
m.	minor	—	the same intonation as the piano
maj.	major		
meas.	measure		

Part I

EARLY SYSTEMS

_____

Chapter 1.   TARTINI AND CAMPAGNOLI

1.1   Resultant tones and contrary tunings

Present concepts of good intonation have evolved from methods used during the past two hundred and fifty years.   One early method stems from the teachings of Giuseppe Tartini,[1] who instructed many fine violinists in Italy starting in 1728.   Tartini taught his pupils to practice major and minor thirds and sixths in double-stops while listening for "third tones" lying in the bass register (see Appendix I).   This resulted in major scales with low major thirds and sixths, flatter than those notes of our piano.

During Tartini's time, keyboard instruments were occasionally tuned with equal temperament; such tunings conflicted with Tartini practices.   By the nineteenth century, equal temperament's new standards already had started to replace Tartini intonations.   This evolutionary process was aided by another tuning scheme introduced by Campagnoli, the great violinist.   It is because of the complete change of standards that resulted by the twentieth century that I regard Tartini tunings as outmoded.   Other objections will be noted later in this chapter.

Giuseppe Tartini

From an engraving by Antonio Brunetti in Franz Farga's Violins & Violinists, trans. by Egon Larsen (London: Rockliff, 1950), facing p. 145. Used by permission of Albert Müller Verlag A. G.

Equal temperament's growing popularity during the nineteenth century influenced the Broadwoods piano-making firm of London to adopt such tunings for all of their pianos, commencing in 1846.[2] Through investigation this statement will prove true, and the belief that Bach invented equal temperament will be disproved.[3] Despite the increased use of equal temperament and Campagnoli's principles during the nineteenth century, however, many violinists continued to follow Tartini's teachings. They applied his tunings to all types of music.

1.2 Disadvantages

Today, our intonation standards are different from Tartini's, and that is my main objection to the current use of his principles, as already stated. Other objections follow.

It is extremely time-consuming and tedious to listen for Tartini's third tones, because their volume is weak. Therefore, practice sessions require utmost privacy without interference from outside conflicting sounds.

'Cello and bass players consider it impractical to listen for third tones ranging in the leger lines below the bass stave. Singers and wind instrumentalists, who emit but a single sound at one time, can listen for third tones only when performing duets.

Since Tartini's major third is flatter than the piano's major third, such intonation--when used melodically--positions the third far away from the perfect fourth. The large-sized semitone that results is contrary to Leopold Auer's teachings. He said:

> Faulty intonation in the case of the half-steps--a very prevalent vice--is a menace against which you must especially be on your guard. If the half-steps are not sufficiently near each other, their intonation will always be dubious. Neglect of the half-step progressions is at the very root of poor intonation....[4]

To achieve small semitones, Auer's students and present string artists have played major thirds as sharp as the piano's, often sharper. In this way, the interval between the third and the fourth becomes smaller (see chart on page 10, laboratory tests in Chapter 5, and chart at the end of Chapter 6).

Tartini's third is the flattest major third that the ear will tolerate. The chart will show that one would have to play the E only slightly flatter than Tartini's to find oneself on the threshold of E♭; audiences regard this as "out-of-tune."

An example of this faulty intonation occurred at a 1980 rehearsal of the New York Philharmonic, during which three wind instrumentalists sustained a major chord. One of the players emitted the chord's major third slightly flatter than Tartini's measurement. Zubin Mehta, the conductor, asked the player to raise the false tuning. The request was complied with, but Mehta--still dissatisfied--asked that the tuning be raised even more. Finally, after a second sharpening was effected, good intonation resulted.

This incident proved three points. First, the out-of-tune player was unaware that today's standards require a raised major third. Second, the conductor--similar

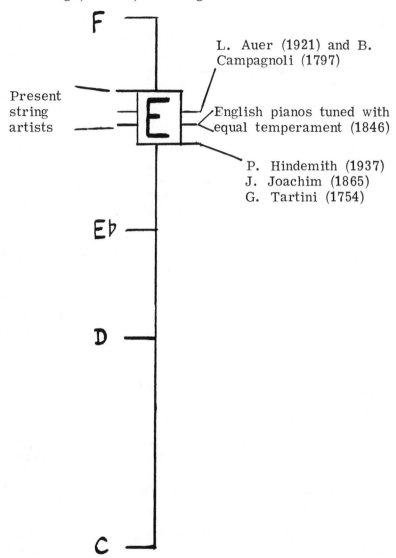

The Evolution of Major-Third Tunings

to an audience--heard the falsity, whereas the player did not. Third, it was dangerous that the player aimed at the Tartini major third, for when played slightly flat, it sounded out-of-tune.

Tartini's tunings do not allow enough leeway for small intonation falsities, which occur occasionally. According to the preceding chart, there is much leeway above the Tartini tuning, but none below it. When one considers that Tartini tunings involve not only major thirds but also minor thirds, minor sixths, and major sixths, it becomes apparent that chances of error are great when using these borderline intonations.

A final reason for rejecting Tartini tunings concerns musicians' careers that have been impeded because of poor intonation; many of these musicians believed firmly in Tartini principles. Thus, it is evident that even though Tartini tunings are correct scientifically they offer too many disadvantages to performing musicians. One of the twentieth century's most noted acoustical musicologists, James Murray Barbour, stated, "Just [Tartini] intonation is a very limited, cumbersome and unsatisfactory tuning system."[5]

1.3 Raised tunings of sharps

Bartolommeo Campagnoli (1751-1827) studied violin with Pietro Nardini, the ablest pupil of Tartini. Thus, in his early years, Campagnoli used Tartini's "third sound" to test intonation accuracy when performing double-stops.[6] He evidently rejected this practice later, for in a second book (dated 1797), he stressed that sharps were to be played higher than enharmonic flats.[7] This means that Campagnoli played G♯ higher than A♭.

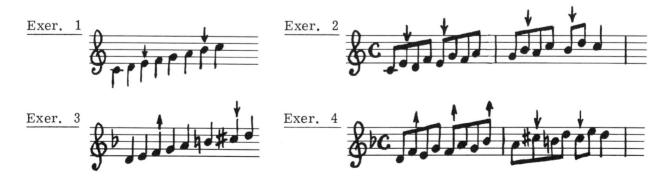

Ex. 1   G♯ — A♭ Present pianos

This practice is still observed today (see Chapter 4). Campagnoli was the very first to write a violin method endorsing that type of intonation,[8] and in so doing provided a drawing of the violin's fingerboard.[9]

Another Campagnoli drawing indicated the tunings of a diatonic scale in which whole-tones were large-sized, semitones small.[10] Auer endorsed such semitones.

1.4 Experimenting with false intonations

Tartini's pupils were not taught to use the small semitones advocated by Campagnoli and Auer. Rather--as will be seen in Exercises 1 and 3--Tartini semitones were large-sized. Arrows over notes indicate Tartini tunings, all of which may be used in the following experiment. First, increase the tempo of the exercises. Second, record the performance on tape.

Exer. 1

Exer. 2

Exer. 3

Exer. 4

Bartolommeo Campagnoli

Copy of 1778 engraving.   Used by permission of Wurlitzer-Bruck Music, New York.

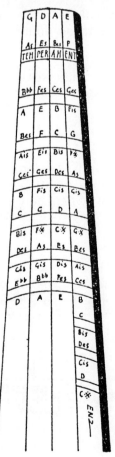

Campagnoli's Drawing of a Violin Fingerboard

(showing raised intonations of sharps and lowered intonations of flats).   From Adolphe Poth, De ontwikkelingsgang der vioolmethodes tot omstreeks 1850 ('s-Gravenhage: W. P. van Stockum, 1949), p. 110.   Used by permission of W. P. van Stockum en Zoon N.V., The Hague.

Third, listen to the playback, a method by which one can hear the false tunings as an audience would. Particularly in fast tempos, audiences (who listen objectively) judge tunings more easily than some players themselves.

NOTES

1. Giuseppe Tartini, Trattato di musica secondo la vera scienza dell' armonia (Padua, 1754). The date of publication was stated erroneously as 1745 by William Pole in his book The Philosophy of Music, 6th ed. (New York, 1924), p. 220. Earlier editions also contained the error.

2. Percy Scholes, The Oxford Companion to Music, 7th rev. ed. (London, New York, and Toronto, 1947), p. 925.

3. In his book Tuning and Temperament (East Lansing, 1951), p. 45, James Murray Barbour stated that Giovanni Mario Lanfranco (fl. 1533) provided the first tuning rules containing characteristics of equal temperament.

4. Leopold Auer, Violin Playing as I Teach It (New York, 1921), p. 94.

5. James Murray Barbour, "Just Intonation Confuted," Music and Letters, XIX (January 1938), p. 48.

6. Bartolommeo Campagnoli, A New Method for the Violin (London, no date), pp. 17 and 125, numbers 237 and 238.

7. Bartolommeo Campagnoli, Metodo per violino (Milan, 1797). See also David D. Boyden, The History of Violin Playing from Its Origins to 1761 (London, 1965), p. 371.

8. David D. Boyden, "Prelleur, Geminiani and Just Intonation," Journal of the American Musicological Society, IV, 3 (Fall 1951), p. 212, footnote 19.

9. Adolphe Poth, De ontwikkelingsgang der vioolmethodes tot omstreeks 1850 ('s-Gravenhage, 1949), p. 110.

10. Bartolommeo Campagnoli, Metodo della meccanica progressiva per suonare il violino (Milan, no date), Table II. This is also cataloged as Nouvelle méthode de la mechanique progressive du jeu de violon, Op. a 21 (Milan, no date).

Chapter 2. THE INTERVAL SYSTEM

[Winds and singers may omit Sections 2, 3, 5, 6, 7, 10.]

2.1 Enlarging and reducing intervals

If you turn the arrows associated with Tartini principles in the opposite direction, your intonation is greatly improved. That is precisely what Campagnoli did:

I have termed this practice the "Interval System"; its first rule is as follows. All intervals that bear an adjective indicating expansion, must be enlarged in size. Thus, in Exercise 5, above, C to D and D to E are major seconds, and each of these major seconds must be spread apart.

Ex. 2

D   E

↕ ↕

C   D

Likewise, F to G, G to A, and A to B are similarly treated.

The second rule, quite the opposite, states that <u>all intervals having an adjective describing reduction of size, should be contracted</u>. Since "minor" indicates contraction, E to F, a minor second should be squeezed together; also B to C. There are actually fourteen intervals within an octave that are affected by the two rules. Following are the abbreviations used:

M. = major, m. = minor, dim. = diminished, aug. = augmented.

Ex. 3

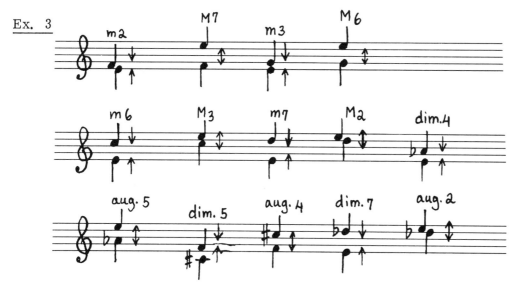

Minor, Major, Diminished, and Augmented Intervals

It can be seen that the word "diminished" suggests contraction, whereas "augmented" suggests expansion.

How do players who use the Interval System solve problems in the following passage?

Ex. 4

They test very little and follow the two rules: major intervals should be large, minor intervals small. While these musicians practice slowly, their minds regulate intonation in the following manner:

Exer. 9

[Winds and singers see Appendix II, then proceed to Section 2.4.]

Observing such alterations, violinists who use the Interval System are able to perform Example 4 satisfactorily. The only tests they make are [musical notation] with the open E string, [musical notation] with the open G string, and [musical notation] with the open D string.

The question "How large should violinists make a major second so that it will sound in tune?" can be answered by taking the following steps. First, guarantee the pitch of the open strings.

2.2   Another way to tune the violin

1)   Tune your violin to the usual perfect fifths. To ensure that the fifths are perfect, play the harmonic [musical notation] on the E string in the fourth position. Test it with the harmonic [musical notation] played with the first finger on the A string--also in the fourth position. Next, play [musical notation] again with the fourth finger; compare it with [musical notation] played with the first finger on the D string. Then follow up with [musical notation] on the D string and [musical notation] on the G string. Now your violin is tuned to absolute perfect fifths.

2.3   Matching large-sized major seconds and thirds with harmonics.

2)   Play the harmonic [musical notation] on the G string, then the open A string [musical notation] . The interval between these two notes is naturally a major second, more often called a "whole-tone." Next, play the harmonic [musical notation] and then the

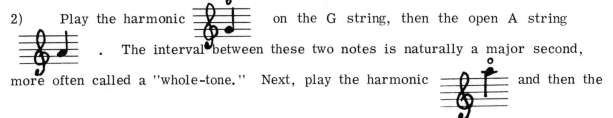

harmonic 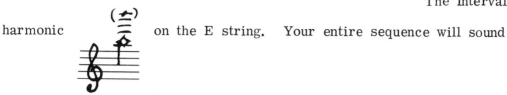 on the E string. Your entire sequence will sound

Exer. 10

Even though you jump octaves, you will hear excellent intonation of G, A, and B. Note that major seconds are large sized.

3)   Following are the same-sized whole-tones as they occur in other areas on the violin's fingerboard. First, play ♪ on the D string. Test it either with the harmonic ♪ on the G string or with the open G string itself. Then play the second finger ♪ , comparing it with the open A string. Next, place the third finger on ♪, and play it with the same intonation as the harmonic ♪, which sounds two octaves higher in range. Practice the following:

Exer. 11

Exer. 12

2.4 Major thirds for brass and strings

In the above exercises, the B's were higher than those Tartini advocated. Fine brass players, who are aware of such differences, raise the low major thirds found in the harmonic series of their instruments. Thus, if a trumpet were pitched in G, the intonation of B in the harmonic series would be identical to the low Tartini tuning found in the Exercise 13--as played on the violin.

Exer. 13

John Ware, first trumpeter of the New York Philharmonic, states that he usually plays the third of the harmonic series with a fingering that sharpens the intonation.[1] In this manner, he can duplicate the tunings of the string section. The Philharmonic's first trombonist, Edward Herman, raises the major third by shortening the slide. When he is practicing fast arpeggios in one position, it is conspicuous that his right hand quickly pulls in on the slide for the major third. Then, the slide is pushed back immediately for the other notes.[2] Such are the standards of fine brass players and others in first-ranking symphony orchestras.

For years, violinists in the top symphony orchestras have led the way in raising major thirds. Since violinists must continue these intonations, it is valuable to practice the following exercises and make comparisons as indicated:

Exer. 14

Keep playing large-sized whole-tones:

Exer. 15

[Winds and singers proceed to Section 2.8.]

2.5 Descending whole-tones for violinists

The next step concerns large-sized whole-tones that descend. After playing the fourth finger, pull the third and second fingers back. Match the intonation of the solid notes in measure 2 with the intonation of the natural harmonics in measure 1.

In the following exercises, pull the first finger as far back as possible:

A very small semitone (minor second) has been created between F and E. Also the major seconds, A to G and G to F, became large sized.

2.6 Danger zones and speed for strings

Exercises 14 to 20 contain quarter- and half-notes, indicating a moderate tempo. If the speed were increased, however, the tunings would be changed, a procedure to be discussed.

Some intonations sound fine in slow or moderate speeds. Yet, when the same intonations are used in faster speeds, they often sound "out of tune." This phenomenon becomes apparent in the following experiment.

As you increase the speed of Exercise 21, gradually play the first finger higher; then gradually lower the first finger.   Record it on tape and listen to the playback.

Exer. 21

At this brisk tempo, the F sounds most in tune when it is played very low.   If you find this passage or a similar one in a fast composition, you will probably practice very slowly at first.   But it should be realized that the final performance will be rendered at a fast speed.   Therefore, when practicing slowly, lower the F very much. Then it will sound "in tune" when played fast.

Practice the following scale slowly, but use large whole-tones and small semi-tones:

Exer. 22

2.7   Limitation of space between violinists' fingers

When the semitone occurs between the third finger and the open string, there is no problem:

Ex. 5

When the semitone falls between two adjacent fingers, however, you must strive to press these two fingers together:[3]

Ex. 6

Now play an F major scale. First, test  with the open E string

. Then play the second finger, F, very close to the 1st finger:

Exer. 23

The first finger, when played on the A and E strings, should be very flat, as it was

in Exercise 21. In this way, you will emit small semitones between and

. Large-sized fingers may have difficulties playing the uppermost range

of Exercise 23, where a minor second occurs between the third and fourth fingers.
Practice will usually master this problem.

When descending from the peak of Exercise 23, the fourth finger of a small
hand--if used on the notes E and A--will experience difficulty. The stretch between
the first and fourth fingers is not easy.

Exer. 24

2.8 Application for strings, winds, and singers

In the following études, minor thirds and minor seconds are small, both when ascending and descending. Practice slowly while analyzing. Then, increase the speed and
exaggerate the intonations indicated by arrows. Etude 2 should be practiced in the
third position; then in the first position.

Etude 1

Lento-Mod^{to}

T. Podnos

Etude 2

Largo-Andante

T. Podnos

2.9 Two types of semitones and the major sixth

In Etudes 1 and 2 you confronted new situations:

Ex. 7

Our Western language terms these intervals "semitones"--it is true--but, in intonation, they are regarded differently. Each of these intervals is spread apart and brings forth a ruling of its own: When two notes comprise a semitone, but bear the same scale name, they must be distant from each other. For instance, E♭ and E♮ both bear the scale name E and therefore must be spread apart. If the notes were written D♯ and E, then only would you compress the minor-second interval. This situation will be explained further in the chapter describing the Accidental System.

Thus far, seconds and thirds have been stressed, because they form the nucleus of all intonation problems. When surmounted by additional seconds or thirds, intervals ranging from fourths to octaves result. The following discussion includes sixths and sevenths.

You already know that a major sixth is formed by the first two notes of "My Bonnie Lies over the Ocean:"

Beginning students should not be misled by the minor sixth found in the first inversion of a major chord: . Only the root position contains the major sixth:

[Winds and singers proceed to Section 2.11.]

2.10 Tuning major sixths to violin harmonics

To hear the major sixth that conforms to present intonation standards, listen again to particular natural harmonics and open strings as your guides.

First, tune your strings accurately, according to the procedure mentioned earlier. Then, play a G harmonic on the G string followed by the open E string:

. The large size of this major sixth is most desirable. Also large sized,

the two harmonics

Exer. 25

played on the D and E strings, respectively, comprise another major sixth. Practice the following:

Exer. 26

Exer. 27

All of these major sixths are larger sized than those that Tartini advocated.

2.11 Intervals and enharmonicism for strings, winds, and singers

In the following exercises, complement the large major sixths with small minor thirds:

Exer. 28

For violinists

1st position

Exer. 29

For everyone

To continue, minor sixths and minor sevenths are compressed, whereas major sevenths are expanded. Etude 3 contains all of these intervals. Diminished fifths should be reduced in size, but augmented fourths should be spread apart. Semitone clusters are treated thus:

Exer. 30

When playing in a fast speed, boldly play enharmonic sequences in this manner:

Exer. 31

In measures 14 and 15 of the following étude, the different intonations of D♯ and E♭ will sound fine as long as you maintain motion.[4] Increase the tempo gradually from Lento to Allegro.

2.12   Disadvantages

The Interval System is extremely helpful, yet it has its shortcomings. If you were tacet for two measures while playing in an ensemble, and then had to "make your

Etude 3

Lento-Allegro

T. Podnos

entrance" by playing the double-stop: , how would you know which note to alter? Your advance knowledge told you that a minor third should be small-sized, but the Interval System provided no clue as to whether you should keep the A♭ fixed and raise the F, or whether you should stabilize the F and lower the A♭. In addition, there were many melodic passages containing similar problems.

Seeking a solution to these situations, many performers have resorted to a practice called the "Accidental System."

NOTES

1. John Ware, conversation with the author, 1980.

2. Discussions about numerous fingerings and slide adjustments for all brass instruments are contained in Chester Roberts's valuable article "Elements of Brass Intonation," The Instrumentalist (March 1975), pp. 86-90.

3. See finger displacement, Chapter 3.

4. For further discussions of enharmonicism, see Chapter 17.

Chapter 3. THE ACCIDENTAL SYSTEM AND FIVE-NOTE[1]
GRAVITATION (Magnetism)

[Winds and singers may omit Section 4.]

3.1 Graphic aids to intonation; tonality and atonality

Performers have no occasion to use the Accidental System when playing music containing only the seven diatonic notes of C major; that scale has no accidentals. In G major, however, violinists raise F♯, and in F major they lower B♭. Thus, the rule of this system is: Exaggerate intonations in the direction indicated by accidentals.

Exercise 32 has four sharps, each of whose pitch should be raised:

Exer. 32

In A♭ major four notes must be lowered:

Exer. 33

Use of the Accidental System is very advantageous in the key of D harmonic minor, which has both flats and sharps:

Exer. 34

29

The Accidental System benefits you mostly because of its graphic nature. In the last exercise sharps are as conspicuous as warning signs along our highways. When using the Interval System, discussed previously, you had to determine which type interval was present and only then would you know what alteration to make. Graphic sharps and flats, on the other hand, provide you with immediate information; this feature is particularly valuable in fast tempos, which allow little time for calculations.

The Accidental System is also a great aid when playing both atonal and tonal music--when "reading at sight":

Exer. 35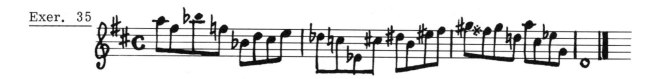

Naturals (♮) play a double role, for when they appear in the flatted keys, they indicate that the intonation must be raised (see Exercise 36); in keys with sharps, contrarily, notes affixed with naturals must be played lower (see Exercise 37):

Exer. 36

Exer. 37

3.2 Semitone clusters and magnetism

Next to be discussed are those cases that contain clusters of semitones, such as:

Ex. 8

which was briefly mentioned in Chapter 2. Since E♭ is lowered and C♯ raised, it appears that both of these notes are attracted to D. Furthermore, this attraction becomes greater in proportion to the gradual increase of tempo. I call such pull "gravitation" or "magnetism."

The force that D has for adjacent semitones is a discovery, perhaps new to musicology and acoustical science.[2] In its simplest form, you can easily discern a central note surrounded by two adjacent semitones, as in Example 8. Some melodies contain two or three central notes, each embraced by two adjacent semitones:

If you find five different central notes, each flanked by two adjoining semitones, you could term the intonational forces "five-note gravitation." The following example in C major has five central notes--C, D, E, G, and A--arranged as follows: C to D = Major second, D to E = Major second, E to G = minor third, G to A = Major second. When ascending ultimately to the octave, the last interval, A to C, would be a minor third. Each one of these central notes is embraced by two adjacent semitones (indicated with small letters):

Ex. 9   Five-Note (Pentatonic) Gravitation (I)

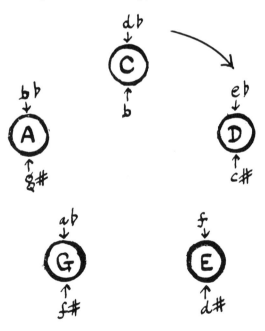

Such semitones, which are attracted, always have scale names that differ from the name of the central note. Thus, C attracts d♭, whose designation, D, is dissimilar from the central note's name. C never attracts c♯, because that note belongs to D♮. The other affiliate, b, clings upward to the central note, C. Identical situations exist with the other four central notes and their adjacent semitones, respectively.

Perhaps a coincidence only, these characteristics are similar to the laws of electricity and physics: opposites attract, likes repel.

3.3 Magnetism in repertory

Play Exercise 38 slowly; then play it faster with exaggerated intonations. When each cluster occurs, its members must huddle together, as previously mentioned.

In addition to semitones attracted by central notes, there are semitones that repel each other. You will find this type, for example, when playing F♭ to F♮ or when playing F♮ to F♯. These three notes--F♭, F♮, and F♯--all have the common scale name of F. And, since "likes repel," the semitone-combinations F♭ to F♮ or F♮ to F♯ should be large sized. Thus, in measures 1 and 2 of Exercise 39, spread apart the semitone F♯ to F♮. Another large semitone exists in measures 4 and 5 that contain a high E and a low E♭.[3]

If you observe the aforementioned principles fully, you could also apply them, perhaps, when playing a chromatic scale:

Chromatic passages are often atonal, particularly in fast tempos. This indicates that chromaticism affects tonality either slightly or not at all. I, personally, use the alterations of Exercise 40 only when playing at moderate speeds.

In quartet repertoire, passages occur frequently that involve central notes and their affiliates. Application of the Accidental System will improve your rendition of the following excerpts:

Exer. 41 String Quartet
Movement IV
Measures 114-115   Measure 179   Ludwig van Beethoven
                                                Op. 18, No. 1

Additional aspects of magnetism will be featured in other sections of this book.

[Winds and singers proceed to Section 3.5.]

3.4 Finger displacement for violinists

Violinists with broad fingers sometimes find it difficult to squeeze their fingertips together, a technique necessary when playing small semitones--as mentioned earlier:

Ex. 10 Compressed Fingers

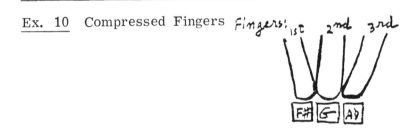

Carl Flesch stated that it is practically impossible to play minor seconds in tune because of the anatomy of the hand.[4] Yet, many violinists with wide fingers solve this problem by lifting up one finger instantaneously to make room for the finger being placed down:

Ex. 11 Finger Displacement

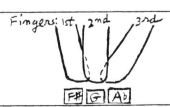

This technique is also used by violinists with small fingers when playing the above semitones in the upper positions of the fingerboard.

3.5 A second magnetic field, for everyone

In addition to the five-tone structure mentioned previously, there is another one in C major: C, D, <u>F</u>, G, A. The adjacent semitones are again included:

<u>Ex. 12</u> Five-Note (Pentatonic) Gravitation (II)

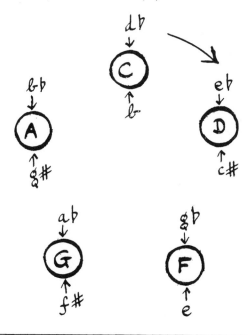

Practice the second set slowly at first; then make the semitones cling to their central notes as the speed increases (see page 32). Incorporate all you have learned thus far in the following études. Arrows are provided sparingly.

NOTES

1. In his article "Notes or Tones?--A Lost Opportunity," <u>Monthly Musical Record</u>, LXXVI, 881 (November 1946), pp. 203-207, Llewelyn S. Lloyd stated, regretfully, that there was a tendency to limit the meaning of "note" to a symbol on a music page. He urged that other writers employ the word "note" also to describe the sound represented by a symbol.

Lloyd used "note" a third way, for in his book Intervals, Scales and Temperaments, edited by Hugh Boyle (London, 1963), p. 151, he referred to the finger keys of keyboard instruments as "white or black notes."

According to tradition, today's musicians regard a musical sound as a note, a circumstance that prompts me to use that term for better comprehension.

2. In his Art of Violin Playing, Book I (New York, 1924), p. 22, Carl Flesch stressed that G♭ should be played very close to F and that F♯ should be played very close to G. However, he did not state that those tunings were to be exaggerated in fast passages.

3. For other discussions concerning the two kinds of semitones, see Christine Heman, Intonation auf Streichinstrumenten (Basel, 1964), pp. 34-35, and Willi Apel, Harvard Dictionary of Music, 2nd ed. (Cambridge, 1975), p. 762.

4. Carl Flesch, The Art of Violin Playing (New York, 1924), Book I, p. 20. Contrary to Flesch's statement, electronic analysis of two performing trios--members of the Boston Symphony Orchestra--revealed that small-sized semitones were preferred to large ones. Of thirty-eight semitones analyzed in slow music, twenty-seven measured smaller than those of the piano. These findings were reported by Charles Shackford, "Some Aspects of Perception," Part II, Journal of Music Theory (April 1962), p. 71.

Fritz Kreisler

Etude 4

Allegretto

T. Podnos

Etude 5

Allegretto

T. Podnos

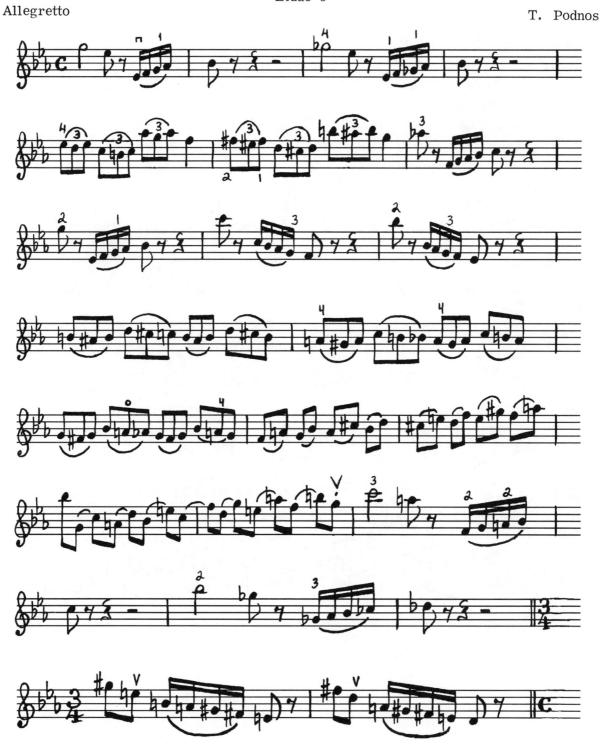

Etude 5 (cont'd.)

Part II

EPISODE

_____

Chapter 4.   SCIENTIFIC ASPECTS

[Winds and singers may omit Section 3.]

4.1   General

This chapter summarizes numerous points discussed thus far and provides extra information to those people interested in musicological aspects of this study.

I use the term "five-note," which musicologists call <u>pentatonic</u>, deriving from the Greek word <u>penta</u> for "five." As you probably noticed in the last chapter, the five-note structure C, D, E, G, A was a gapped scale. It had no semitones; it had only whole-tones and one minor third if you discounted the added C an octave higher than the root. Thus, a pentatonic melody with an octave range (C, D, E, G, A, C) would include two minor thirds.

4.2   Pentatonicism, the basis of tonality

In our Western culture, it has been said that the pentatonic scale was basic and that our diatonic scale gradually evolved from it. The pentatonic scale was supplemented with two passing notes, the new structure then being regarded as 5 + 2. But pentatonic melodies have persisted in the midst of all other changes that have occurred in our music. Popular melodies, such as "Who," "Dinah," "Louise," and "My Blue Heaven," contain much pentatonicism, and thus may be partially played on the black keys of the piano. Stemming from black influences in the southern part of the United States are those melodies "Nobody Knows the Trouble I've Seen," "Old Folks at Home," "Ol' Man River," and the Largo from Dvořák's New World Symphony, all of which are either partly or wholly pentatonic. You are well acquainted with "Old MacDonald Had a Farm," "Mary Had a Little Lamb," "Auld Lang Syne," and "Comin' Through the Rye." Actually, pentatonic melodies may be found in numerous areas of the world, a fact that supports the belief that much indigenous music has five tones for its foundation.

[Winds and singers proceed to Section 4.4.]

4.3 Pentatonicism and string intonation

As pointed out in Chapter 3, intonation is closely related to pentatonic structures. We will discuss that bond further.

First, play an E major scale at a very fast speed:

Exer. 42

Then play an E pentatonic scale having the same rhythm, but repeat the indicated pentatonic notes instead of using the diatonic 5 + 2 structure of Exercise 42:

Exer. 43

Now alternate those two exercises in an exceedingly fast tempo:

Exer. 44

In either case there is no threat to tonality as there would be in using Tartini's low G♯ and D♯.

True, the identical rhythmic pattern helps to provide a link between the sequences, but do you hear an illusion? Because of the fast speed, G♯ and D♯ have clung closely to and gradually become part of A and E, respectively. This strange phenomenon requires further investigation by scientists.

4.4 Contrasting wind intonation to sensitive string intonation

Following is a different situation that concerns musical intonation. Woodwind and brass instruments contain many inherent tunings that are false. Manufacturers and skilled craftsmen attempt to instill equally tempered pitches in those instruments but have not met with complete success.[2] To alter intonations, all wind instrumentalists resort to either different fingerings, making fingerholes wider or narrower, extension of slides, or "humoring" of intonations (in which the position of the lips is altered). Fortunately, wind players need concern themselves mostly with tunings performed in slow tempos or in stationary moments found in ensemble playing. The audience seldom hears faulty tunings of flutists or trumpeters when those musicians render fast scales notated in sixteenth- or thirty-second-notes.

To the contrary, faulty intonation in string performances of fast music is very noticeable. Violinists and cellists must constantly police their tunings in all tempos. It remains for future acousticians to provide scientific reasons why violinists have to be more critical of their intonations than wind players do in moving passages.

Thus, string players will benefit the most from this book. In the category of slow or moderate speeds, wind players and singers benefit to a lesser degree. Yet, Dr. Hugh Ross--conductor of the New York Schola Cantorum--states that vocalists could apply such principles to great advantage.[3]

The Interval and Accidental Systems have several common characteristics. In A major, for instance, tunings of the third, sixth, and seventh steps are raised in both systems. These major intervals, when measured from the scale's root, have large dimensions. You could also treat the following intervals identically in both systems:

Ex. 13

4.5 Measuring intervals mathematically

A misconception exists that such tuning characteristics were formed during the period when accidentals became abundant in musical composition: A.D. 1400-1600. Actually, Pythagoras provided mathematical measurements for many types of intervals as early as 532 B.C. "Pythagorean Intonation," a common term among musicologists, includes the same traits as those of the Interval System. Campagnoli did not conceive Pythagorean Intonation; he did apply its principles to violin playing.[4]

In order to facilitate understanding of Pythagorean Intonation, you will want to know of a method for measuring intervals devised by Alexander J. Ellis during the later nineteenth century.[5] He gave the interval C-C♯ a value of 100. Likewise, C♯-D, another semitone, was also given the value 100. To arrive at the value for the wholetone C-D, you merely had to add C-C♯ and C♯-D: 100 + 100. In this way, the reading for C-D became 200. Ellis formulated those readings in conformance with the tunings of our piano, equal temperament. He continued to add 100 for each semitone and arrived finally at the octave with the reading 1200; there are twelve semitones in the octave.

Scientific Aspects / 45

Pythagoras, from a fresco by Raphael
Used by permission of Yeshiva University.

4.6 Cents measurement

In the following example, you will see that each semitone equals 100, and their sums
are computed by additions of these:

Ex. 14   TABLE I: Equal Temperament Measured in Cents

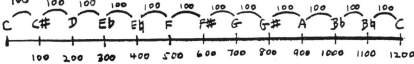

Intervals:

Sums:

Ellis continued further by calling his method "Cents measurement." He transformed vibrations-per-second readings into Cents readings by using a logarithmic procedure. [6] If a violist tuned the C string to the piano's C and then played a C♯ on the "sharp side," the reading for this intonation would be greater than 100 Cents. Depending on the extent of sharpening of this C♯, the Cents value could vary any place between 100 and 150. However, 150 Cents would be so sharp that it would fall exactly halfway between the piano's C♯ and D; musicologists regard that sound as neutral intonation, but most people call it "out of tune." These neutral intonations are sometimes called "sour notes." Accordingly, musicians who accidentally render Tartini's major third on the "flat side" often produce a neutral third of 350 Cents.

Tartini's major third, 386 Cents, at which he arrived by testing for resultant tones, was 14 Cents flatter than the piano's major third of 400 Cents. Moreover, Tartini's 386 Cents was 22 Cents flatter than the Pythagorean major third of 408 Cents commonly heard in performances of today's finest musicians.

Table II contains Cents values for all of Pythagoras' tunings. Thus, Pythagorean Intonation can be indicated accurately by numerals, whereas the Interval System merely guides you in using large- or small-sized intervals.

Musicologists have termed Tartini's tunings "just," because Tartini's tests involved natural overtones, such as the small major third of 386 Cents already discussed; scientists call that tuning "acoustically correct." But, to musicians, Tartini's "just" tunings are often troublemakers. For that reason, many artists have rejected these tunings and have replaced them with other tunings already described.

The following table first depicts different tunings of a C major diatonic scale, while the section on the right side of the page contains three types of tunings: chromatic, equally tempered, and Pythagorean.

Observe five other characteristics, 1) Within the octave there are thirty-three tunings, which derive from equally tempered and Pythagorean measurements. 2) If a piano were tuned in absolute perfect fifths--C, G, D, A, E, B, F♯, C♯, G♯, D♯, A♯, E♯, and B♯--the final B♯ would exceed the original C by 23.46 Cents. This interval from C up to B♯ is called "the Pythagorean comma" and has the ratio 531441:524288. To correct this excess, piano tuners make each perfect fifth smaller in size. Equal temperament thereby contains fifths that are not absolutely perfect like the tunings of violin strings. 3) The chart excludes decimals for all Cents readings, with the exception of the Pythagorean comma, 23.46 Cents. 4) In Pythagorean Intonation, semitones with scale names that are different, D♯-E, measure 90 Cents. Semitones with scale names that are similar, D♮-D♯, read 114 Cents. Referring back to

Example 8 and subsequent discussions, it becomes clear that there are

two kinds of semitones, each with its own tuning requirements. 5) All of Pythagoras' major and augmented intervals are large sized, whereas minor and diminished intervals are small. From this standpoint, the three systems--Interval, Accidental, and Pythagorean--are somewhat similar and, thus, are all conducive to good intonation.

The Interval and Accidental Systems, as already pointed out, have deficiencies. Because of this circumstance, there arises the need for a system that will compensate for such shortcomings (see Chapters 6-16).

TABLE II

Cents Measurement of Intervals

Equal Temperament	Pythagorean Intonation	Equal Temperament	Pythagorean Intonation
Diatonic		Chromatic	
1200 C	1200	1200 C	B# 1223.46 / C 1200
1100 B	1110 High Leading Tone	1100 B,Cb	B 1110 / Cb 1086
		1000 A#,Bb	A# 1020 / Bb 996
900 A	906 Maj. 6th	900 A	A 906
		800 G#,Ab	G# 816 / Ab 792
700 G	702 Perf. 5th	700 G	G 702
		600 F#,Gb	F# 612 / Gb 588
500 F	498 Perf. 4th	500 E#,F	E# 521 / F 498
400 E	408 Maj. 3rd	400 E,Fb	E 408 / Fb 384
		300 D#,Eb	D# 318 / Eb 294
200 D	204 Maj. 2nd	200 D	D 204
		100 C#,Db	C# 114 / Db 90
C		C	B# 23.46 / C

NOTES

1. I have here used one of the forms of the pentatonic scale.

2. Theodor Podnos, "Woodwind Intonation," Woodwind Magazine, II, 4 (December 1949), p. 5.

3. Hugh Ross, letter to the author, 1967.

4. By his time, numerous theorists had already endorsed Pythagorean tunings. See J. Murray Barbour, "The Persistence of the Pythagorean Tuning System," Scripta Mathematica, I, 4 (New York, June 1933), pp. 293-295.

5. Hermann L. F. von Helmholtz, Sensations of Tone..., trans. by Alexander J. Ellis, 4th English ed. (London, 1912), p. 41^n and Appendix XX, Section C, pp. 446-451.

6. See Curt Sachs, The Rise of Music in the Ancient World East and West (New York, 1943), p. 28. See also Robert W. Young's Table Relating Frequency to Cents (Elkhart, 1952).

Chapter 5. LABORATORY TESTS AND DISCOVERIES

[Winds and singers may omit Section 3.]

5.1 Analyses of performing artists

While searching for other forces that control intonation, I carried out tests and analyses of performances by Pablo Casals, Emanuel Feuermann, Jascha Heifetz, and Fritz Kreisler--all of whom have exhibited impeccable intonation. The recordings that were selected contained innumerable examples of intonation used by those artists during the peak of their careers. Music in slow, moderate, and fast tempos was categorized. Then I transferred each performance from the original record to a tape, whose speed could be reduced. Finally, through laboratory procedures, readings were acquired that eventually led to the following observations.

All of these artists used similar tunings in slow tempos. Minor seconds varied approximately between the measurements of equal temperament (100 Cents) and Pythagorean (90 Cents). Major seconds were large sized; major thirds were seldom as small as Tartini's. For all the other intervals, the artists favored Pythagorean intonation, although they occasionally used equal temperament.

When playing allegro compositions, the artists exaggerated beyond Pythagorean measurements. Minor thirds were frequently rendered as small as 290 Cents; major thirds as large as 414 Cents; major sixths, 912 Cents; minor sevenths, as low as 992 Cents; major sevenths, as high as 1117 Cents. Also of great importance was the fact that all these great solo artists used the same kind of intonation independent of each other. Their tunings identify readily with the principles described in the following chapters.

Pablo Casals, whose playing was saturated with Pythagorean characteristics, called his good intonation la justesse expressive. Another famous cello teacher, Diran Alexanian, insisted that his pupils use Pythagorean intonation.

If you wish to examine published findings, refer to works by the following four authors: Paul C. Greene,[1] James F. Nickerson,[2] Ottokar Cadek,[3] and Charles R. Shackford[4]--already mentioned in Chapter 3 (footnote 4). Greene tested intonations

Jascha Heifetz

Used by permission of the Music Division of the New York Public Library at Lincoln Center; Astor, Lenox and Tilden Foundations.

in both slow and fast tempos of six violinists, including the concertmaster of the St. Louis Symphony Orchestra. At the end of Greene's exhaustive discussion, be sure to read his conclusive remarks on page 249. Nickerson's discussions and readings reveal that intonation is governed more by melodic pull than by harmonic pull. Players of six string quartets participated in his tests. Cadek provided a thorough history of violin intonation but neglected to make any laboratory readings. He, like Greene and Nickerson, championed Pythagorean intonation.

Charles Shackford provided laboratory readings of three performing string trios, six of whose members were selected from the Boston Symphony Orchestra. Semitones with different scale names--e.g., F♯-G--sometimes read as small as 82 or 84 Cents.[5] Whole-tones were often played with approximate Pythagorean measurements of 209 or 210 Cents: on other occasions as large as 218, 221, or even 228 cents.[6] See the end of Appendix I for other tests.

5.2 A new system

Another force affecting intonation, in addition to those already discussed, concerns chords and tunings of the notes that comprise such structures. Each note, according to its position in a chord, must be tuned either low, high, or intermediate, as in piano tuning (see Table IV, page 182).

To cite only two examples, the major third of a C major chord should have a raised intonation; D major has a raised F♯. Such tunings were used by the artists mentioned at the beginning of this chapter and by participants in the laboratory tests made by Greene, Nickerson, and Shackford.

Violinists know they have to alter many intonations in various harmonies and in many keys. Actually, there are forty intonations to the octave that violinists use to sound "in tune." If the ear alone is used to determine these tunings, however, it often leads to unsatisfactory results; this "hit or miss" method wastes many hours of practice time. It is more practical to learn a system that will provide accurate tunings.

I studied the violin with eight famous teachers who received their training from either the Russian school, the Hungarian-German (Flesch), the French, the Austrian, or the Belgian. None of them related intonation to chords. It was only through experimentation, independent of my teachers, that I discovered this phenomenon in 1936 and then applied its principles while practicing. After three months of concentration, I knew the proper place for each finger before placing it on the fingerboard, a mental process. Gradually, such thinking became as natural as breathing, and intonation became a lesser problem.

[Winds and singers proceed to Chapter 6.]

5.3 Experiments in fast tempos

Following are some of the observations which resulted in my system, Chordal Intonation.

Play Exercise 45 in both slow and fast tempos:

Exer. 45

There is never a threat to the C tonality, nor is there a threat if you play an entire pentatonic structure:

Exer. 46

Now lower the F in Exercise 45 slightly. When played in a slow tempo, this intonation sounds too high for E. Such tuning, however, produces an excellent E when played fast:

Ex. 15   Tunings in Different Tempos

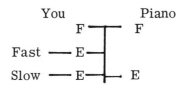

If you record these experiments, you may be pleasantly surprised with the results.

Next, lower the E still further. Such an E sounds fine in slow tempos but is "out of tune" in fast tempos. Moreover, in fast tempos, the last lowered E threatens the C major tonality. A rule resulted: <u>Always play the major third of a major key very sharp in fast tempos.</u> (This means much sharper than the piano tuning.)

Later, tests involving minor keys resulted in a second rule: <u>Play the minor third extremely flat in Allegro music.</u> In slow music, of course, the minor third should be only slightly flatted.

Paul Hindemith, the great composer and theorist, stated, "But why the ... distance between the major and minor thirds should have such extraordinary psychological significance remains a mystery."[7]

I believe that the aforementioned phenomena (Example 15), joined together with those theories that are related to five-note (pentatonic) gravitation--as already discussed in Chapter 3--answer the unsolved question concerning melodic pull on intonation.

My system of Chordal Intonation, which follows, is based on the phenomenon of thirds, but also includes other tunings, all of which play an integral part in musical performances.

NOTES

1. Paul C. Greene, "Violin Performance with Reference to Tempered, Natural, and Pythagorean Intonation," University of Iowa Studies, Psychology of Music, IV (1936), pp. 232-251. See also the same author's article "Violin Intonation," The Journal of the Acoustical Society of America, IX (July 1937), pp. 43-44.

2. James F. Nickerson, "Intonation of Solo and Ensemble Performance of the Same Melody," The Journal of the Acoustical Society of America, XXI, 6 (November 1949), pp. 593-595.

3. Ottokar Cadek, "String Intonation in Theory and Practice." Paper read at the M. T. N. A. -A. S. T. A. String Forum in Chicago, Illinois, January 1, 1949. See also Music Journal, VII, 3 (May-June 1949), pp. 6-7, 37-40.

4. Charles Shackford, "Some Aspects of Perception," Journal of Music Theory, Part I (November 1961), pp. 162-202; Part II (April 1962), pp. 66-90.

5. Ibid., Part II, Example 32, p. 72.

6. Ibid., Examples 33 and 34, pp. 73 and 74.

7. Paul Hindemith, The Craft of Musical Composition, Book I (Mainz, 1937); translated by Arthur Mendel (London, 1942), p. 79.

Part III

CHORDAL INTONATION

THE PRIMARY CHORDS

Chapter 6.   INTONATION AS GOVERNED BY THE TONIC CHORD

[Winds and singers may omit Sections 3 and 5.]

6.1   General

In our Western music, the primary distinction between C minor and C major lies in the third step of those scales: E♭ and E♮. This third step comprises the first discussion.

6.2   Major and minor tonalities contrasted

If you slide your first finger from E♭ to E♮, 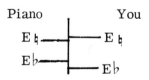 at what point does the sound stop being E♭; and when does it start being E♮? This contingency may prompt you to play these two notes with decided contrast, since each helps to portray a different tonality.   As grief is the opposite of happiness, C minor is the opposite of C major.   Distinguish the two tonalities by playing E♭ slightly lower than the piano's tuning, and E♮ slightly higher.   (Throughout the text, continue to use the piano tuning as a standard from which to deviate.)

Ex. 16   The Nucleus of Chordal Intonation

Piano   You
E ♮ ——————— E ♮
E♭ ——————— E♭

   In Exercises 47 and 48, alterations are indicated by arrows; note that E♮ and E♭ are a large semitone apart.

Exer. 47

Exer. 48

Practice Exercise 49, which follows, and remember to place the second finger very close to the sharpened first finger, thus producing a small minor second:

Exer. 49

By playing the E high and the F low, we have automatically made the major second D to E large in size; also, the major second F to G became enlarged. We have thus conformed with the measurements of Pythagorean intonation.

[Winds and singers proceed to Section 6. 4.]

6. 3   Playing with open strings

What happens when the same notes are played an octave higher?

Exer. 50

First, we find that E occurs on an open string, whose pitch cannot be raised during performance. In this case, lower all the other notes, whereby the E will sound high in relation to them. Violinists contend with identical situations many times, which is the reason for stating this exception now.

Playing Exercise 49 in C minor offers no exceptional problems, since the first finger merely has to be played as low as possible to the nut of the fingerboard:

Exer. 51

If we transpose the same passage to F minor, however, a new problem arises;

the fourth finger must be played very close to the third finger:

Exer. 52

6.4 Minor thirds, major thirds, and piano accompaniment

In both Exercises 51 and 52, we continually lowered the third step, an alteration that contributed to a convincing minor tonality. By realizing the importance of this, we have taken our first step in understanding Chordal Intonation.

We know that the notes C, E, and G comprise the Tonic chord (or triad) of C major and that this chord is indicated by a Roman numeral, I. Regardless of the order in which these three notes occur, the harmony remains the same. Likewise, the major third of the triad is always raised:

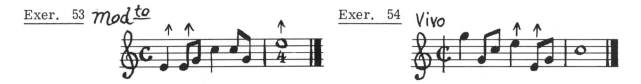

Exer. 53   Exer. 54

We may ask, "What happens when the fourth finger is played higher than the open E string?" The answer would be different for each of the above phrases. In Exercise 53 the final E, which we played for four full beats, would sound fine if we held this note either with sustained piano accompaniment or in a solo phrase. The piano's tuning for this note is slightly flatter, it is true, but the piano's volume decreases immediately after the pianist strikes the finger key. Our E, rendered sharply, contributes to a convincing C major tonality. For proof of this fact, play the following exercise accompanied by a pianist:[1]

Exer. 55

Nickerson's findings of violin performances--previously mentioned--included major thirds that were always pitched sharper than those of equal temperament. In solo performances, violinists who participated in those experiments (ca. 1947-1948) often played major thirds as much as one-tenth of a semitone sharper than the piano's tuning. [2]

Approximately eleven years later, Charles Shackford used advanced electronic equipment and found that selected string instrumentalists of the Boston Symphony Orchestra favored major thirds as large as Nickerson's, sometimes larger. [3] Since all of those readings were taken of slow performances, it now appears that some innate force draws the major third closer to the perfect fourth in all tempos. Another aspect of that study follows.

[Winds and singers proceed to Section 6.6.]

6.5 Speed

Exercise 56, part of the second Kreutzer étude, contains a major third in motion. Practice the beginning measures at a fast tempo using the indicated fingerings and tunings. Then record it in that manner, and listen to the playback.

Rodolphe Kreutzer, Etude No. 2

Braunschweig: Litolff, No. 507, [n.d.].

You will find that--in C major--both the intonation of the open E string and the sharpened intonation of the fourth finger are fully satisfactory; you could call this an auditory illusion. Also note that, in a fast-moving melody, tunings of the major third can vary, providing that they center around the Pythagorean measurement of 408 Cents or slightly higher.

6.6 Analysis before performance

The following exercises contain problems to be solved through analysis. In addition to Chordal Intonation, use the Accidental and Interval Systems.

Exercise 59 is followed by a chart already presented in Chapter 1. The added Cents readings, printed diagonally, conform with evidence just studied. Further explanations may be found on pages 45 to 46.

Exer. 57

Exer. 58

Exer. 59

F# is sharper than Gb

The Evolution of Major-Third Tunings,
with Cents Measurements Added

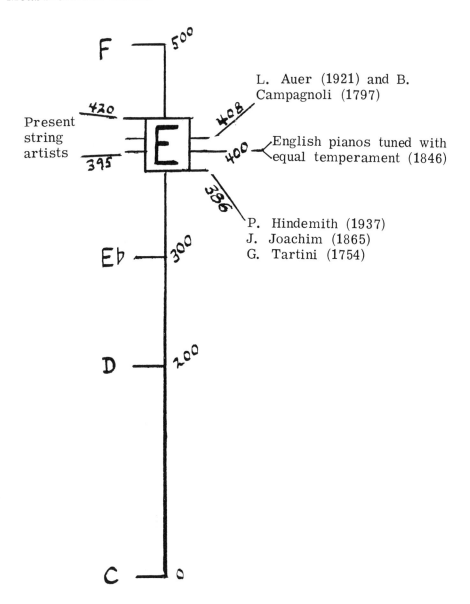

NOTES

1. This test may also be made in C minor. To do this, change all the E♮'s in Exercise 55 to E♭'s, and point all the arrows downward.

2. James F. Nickerson, "Intonation of Solo and Ensemble Performance of the Same Melody," The Journal of the Acoustical Society of America, XXI, 6 (November 1949), p. 594.

3. The Boston players occasionally used major thirds and tenths smaller than those of equal temperament, but usually preferred tunings of 400 to 420 Cents; they even exceeded that range in three instances. Detailed findings were provided by Charles Shackford, "Some Aspects of Perception," The Journal of Music Theory, Part I (November 1961), p. 191.

Chapter 7. THE DOMINANT CHORD

7.1 General

In Chapter 6 we discussed the Tonic chord. We also concerned ourselves with several other circumstances that occur frequently in violin playing; some of these appear when we least expect them. We learned, however, which steps to pursue in those cases involving open strings, big- and small-sized semitones, fast tempos, and different enharmonic intonations.

7.2 Raising the leading tone, the chord's third

The next discussion concerns the Dominant chord, indicated by the Roman numeral V and built on the fifth step of a scale. In the key of G major, for example, the Dominant triad D, F♯, A is treated in the same manner as the Tonic triad; the third is raised. Exercise 60 contains both the I and V harmonies, supplemented with proper arrows. In the third measure, play G very close to the preceding F♯:

Exer. 60

The Dominant chord is usually a major triad regardless of whether the key is major or minor:

Exer. 61

Note that all Tonic bars have a B♭ that must be lowered, whereas all Dominant bars have an F# that must be raised. Also, F# is the leading tone of both G minor and G major; you contribute to the G tonality by raising the intonation of the leading tone, F#. And, of course, you should raise this intonation still further as the tempo increases.

Practice the following exercises three ways: 1) For slow performances; 2) In a slow speed, but containing exaggerated tunings that will sound in tune when played fast (see pages 19-21); 3) In a fast tempo.

Exer. 62

In the following exercises, mark the chord symbols and then the arrows.

Exer. 63

Exer. 64

Exer. 67

To make the open D-string appear sharpened, lower the other notes.

Chapter 8. THE DOMINANT SEVENTH CHORD

8.1 The augmented fourth and diminished fifth

Many composers, when writing the Dominant chord, add the seventh. Thus, in C major the Dominant-seventh chord would sound 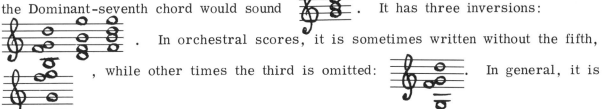 . It has three inversions: . In orchestral scores, it is sometimes written without the fifth, , while other times the third is omitted: . In general, it is readily distinguished from other chords, because it usually includes either an augmented fourth, 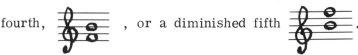 , or a diminished fifth .

8.2 The raised third and lowered minor seventh

We already know that the third of the Dominant chord should be raised. The added seventh, on the other hand, should be lowered. In Exercise 68--played in the first position--the first and second fingers should rub against each other, particularly in fast tempos:

Exer. 68

FOR VIOLINISTS

If you play the second measure in the second position,

Exer. 69

lower the first finger and stretch the fourth finger to play the raised B. The two techniques, rubbing and stretching, require our utmost attention at all times.

FOR EVERYONE

By inverting the above augmented fourth, a diminished fifth results: .

This diminished interval is contracted in size.[1] Complete the arrows and chord symbols yourself in the following exercises:

Exer. 70

Practice Exercises 71 to 73, using the above directions. In measure 2 of Exercise 71, the Dominant chord lacks A, its root:

Exer. 71

Exer. 72

Exer. 73   3rd pos.

8.3 Performing with piano accompaniment

In each key of Classical and Romantic music, the third of the tonic and the third and seventh of the Dominant appear to affect tonality more than the tunings of other tones. Use of the awkward fingerings in the following exercises will give your fingers more agility.

Exer. 74

Exer. 75

Such tunings of the three sensitive tones help us when playing alone or with piano accompaniment. This asset was introduced earlier in Chapter 6, in which our major third, E, produced a small tuning discrepancy with the piano E, which faded. Likewise, when we play Exercise 68 of this chapter in a slow tempo with a pianist playing the indicated chords, our intonations of B and F again ensure good tonality.

When fine violinists play running passages accompanied by intricate piano parts, the two instruments constantly produce tiny tuning differences on E, B, and F. The results must be satisfying, for audiences often respond with hearty applause.

An opposite case exists with the four other notes of C major--C, D, G, and A. These should match keyboard tunings in slow music, particularly in stationary chords. (For intonation in chamber music, see page 152.)

In Etude 6, experiment with a pianist, who will play the chords indicated by guitar symbols.

Etude 6

Alternate between major and minor: slow, then fast

T. Podnos

Etude 7

Major and minor thirds in different tempos. Adjacent semitone embellishments played closely to their central notes (see Chapter 3).

Andante   T. Podnos

In view of the fact that performers have to make the above-described adjustments to acquire better intonation, it is natural that they ask the question, "Why can't we simply use the piano's tunings having but twelve intonations in the octave?" It is true that equal temperament has been used officially as the standard piano tuning since 1846 (as mentioned in Chapter I),[2] but the ratios of this scheme are too intricate for performing musicians. The interval assumed to be a perfect fifth, for example, is slightly contracted: 1/50 of a semitone (see Table II, page 47). A piano tuner will disclose involvement with this and other minute variations throughout the piano's entire range. Equal temperament is a compromise tuning system and has only one perfect interval, the octave.

In violin performances, the Tonic and Dominant chords contain extra-sensitive notes, whereas other chords have notes requiring smaller alterations. Such is the Subdominant.

NOTES

1. Selected string players--including Boston Symphony personnel--play small diminished fifths (the mean being 593 Cents) and large augmented fourths (the mean being 611 Cents), as reported by Charles Shackford, "Some Aspects of Perception," Journal of Music Theory, Part I (November 1961), pp. 201 and 200, Example 29.

2. Related to tuning problems, the pitch level of "A" was also disputed for centuries. Handel's tuning fork was pitched at 422.5 vibrations per second, while Mozart's sounded 421.6; these pitches were nearly a whole-tone lower than the 452.5 "A" accepted by the London Philharmonic during the mid-nineteenth century. See the author's article "And Where Is Your 'A' Today," Woodwind Magazine, I, 2 (December 1948), p. 3. See also Percy Scholes, The Oxford Companion to Music, 7th rev. ed. (London, New York, and Toronto, 1947), p. 732; George Bernard Shaw's valuable article listed under "References Cited"; and the article "Pitch" in Willi Apel's Harvard Dictionary of Music, 2nd ed. (Cambridge, 1970), p. 678.

Chapter 9.   THE SUBDOMINANT CHORD

_____

9.1   Slight tuning alterations

The chord built on the fourth degree of a scale, the Subdominant, is indicated by the Roman numeral IV and occurs as either a major or a minor triad.   The intonations of this harmony deviate but slightly from equal temperament, and require, therefore, arrows with split stems:

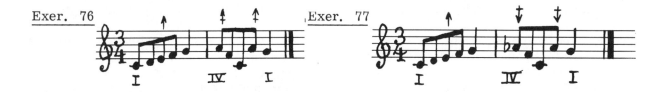

Apparently, the above A's and A♭'s are not as delicate as particular tones of the Tonic and Dominant seventh--an important fact to remember.   In the following exercise, mark a chord symbol under each note; also mark arrows.

9.2   The common tone of the Dominant seventh and Subdominant chords

Now that you marked and practiced Exercise 78, you probably found the G's problematical in measure 9. The first G of the V7 chord was played low, whereas the second G, the root of IV, required no alteration. Consider measure 9 as an exceptional case, whereby you should employ a low G in both harmonies. Consequently, the interval G down to D (in the IV harmony) becomes a small fourth, a falsity usually unnoticed by audiences. (Compare this situation with that of perfect fifths, as discussed in Chapter 18.) This is the rule: The tunings of the Dominant seventh chord are more important than the tunings of the Subdominant. This practice is most helpful in moving passages.

In the next exercise, measure two contains a major Subdominant with a slightly raised B♮. Measure six, the minor Subdominant, has a slightly lowered B♭.

Exer. 79

Analyze and practice Exercises 78 and 79 in both slow and fast speeds. This systematic approach should give you confidence.

Still analyzing in D minor, how would you treat the G's if the IV were followed by the V?

Exer. 80

First, stabilize the G in the second measure. In the third measure, retain the same tuning for G, but raise E and C♯. Your V7 now includes correct relations between its own intervals. The minor third, G to E is small sized; the minor third E to C♯ is small sized; and, most important, the diminished fifth G down to C♯ is automatically small sized, thus contributing to the D tonality.

When you finish this chapter, a major portion of your intonation studies will be completed. Use this knowledge at ensemble rehearsals where you are helped by harmonies and chordal structures. Observe that knowing how to plan intonations before sounding them produces better results than depending on the ear to solve tuning problems.

9.3 The use of different systems

To continue our discussions, Exercise 79 contained many notes belonging to chords already studied. It also included passing notes. Probably, you determined their intonations by using the Interval System. The first two notes of Exercise 79, D to E, a major second, required expansion:

Ex. 17

In measure 3, D to C♯ was a minor second and required contraction. A to B, a major second of measure 7, was large sized. The Interval System helped you to determine correct intonations.

All of these notes could also be analyzed, however, by using a different method, that of Chordal Intonation. Marked first are the chord symbols under each note; then altered intonations are indicated by arrows:

Exer. 81

Each system has its own characteristics. In the Interval System every interval must be computed. Thus, twelve computations were required in Example 17.

When using Chordal Intonation, as indicated in Exercise 81, we are cautious of only six notes; the other notes are performed with piano tunings. Chordal Intonation is thus economical as well as practical.

The following exercises and études omit additional marks. Sitting at a desk, indicate the chords underneath each note; the arrows belong above. Remember the exceptional cases that concern open strings, and IV and V relations. Five-note gravitation concerning "central notes and adjoining semitones" proves useful in relation to the Accidental System. Also, consult the Interval System. Such procedures require care and patience.

In Etude 9--measures 2, 3, 8, 9, and 20--note the appoggiaturas (unprepared suspensions).

Exer. 82

Exer. 83

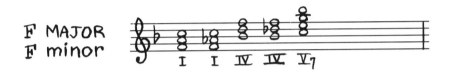

Etude 8

Etude 9

Maestoso   T. Podnos

Chapter 10.   DETERMINATION OF HARMONIES DURING PERFORMANCE

[Winds and singers may omit Section 6.]

10.1   General

In the preceding chapters, chords and arrows were marked down while sitting at a desk.   Then--before playing a phrase--the intonation system providing the best solution was chosen.

10.2   Improvising chords

This lesson shows how to recognize particular harmonies as they occur during performance.   While playing a marching melody such as the following,

Exer. 84

say to yourself, "This is a Tonic chord, this is a Dominant chord."   The second time you play the first beats of these measures, say, "This note is the Tonic's root; this the Dominant's third; this the Dominant's fifth."   During the final playing, realize that the Tonic's root requires no alteration, whereas the Dominant's third does--that of sharpening; the third measure contains the Dominant's fifth (no alteration), and the last measure has the Tonic's root (no alteration).   Diligent practice will make it possible to complete all of these analyses simultaneously.   Although taxing, such mental work gradually becomes second nature.

   The ability to determine harmonies quickly is a common characteristic of musicians who play ballroom engagements.   They know all melodies and can improvise second or third harmonies beneath a melody for an entire evening!

Ex. 18

If you have this talent, application of Chordal Intonation will be easy. In any case, the following procedure may be helpful.

Commence by humming a note that harmonizes with the note already played. That is fine, but it does not provide a full chord. To find a chord in its fundamental position, you must first seek the root. Accomplish that in the following manner. Starting with a given note in the soprano voice, sing or play a harmonizing chord-tone in the alto. Then descend--by intervals of the chord--until two of these intervals equal a perfect fifth; the lower note of this fifth is the root.

10.3 A note common to two chords

This is the printed note: ♪. Do you hear a C chord in your head when playing this note, or do you hear an F chord? If you feel that the proper harmonies should be "G" or "E", then the next chord tone--as you descend--would be "G," ♪, then followed by "E" ♪. When arriving at "C," ♪, observe that the last two intervals comprise a perfect 5th: ♪. "C" is therefore the root. In realizing that this chord is the Tonic of C major, we automatically know that the original given note ♪ should remain unaltered, in conformance with the piano's C.

In the other case, the given note "C" would be related to an F chord. We already sense that "A" harmonizes with "C." As our voices descend, we feel that "F" also sounds in harmony with the given note. We have already arrived at the root, because the interval from the given "C" down to the final "F" is a perfect fifth: ♪. Thus, the intonation of the given note, "C" (the Subdominant's fifth), requires no alteration. If the given note were "A," however, we would sing by intervals in a descending direction until we arrived at "F," a major tenth lower. "A," the third of the IV would be rendered ↑ : ♪. If the given note were "F," we would have a choice of two chords to use in our analysis: 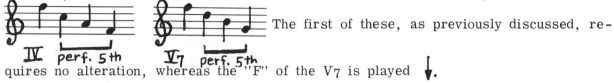 The first of these, as previously discussed, requires no alteration, whereas the "F" of the V7 is played ↓.

Although one may readily grasp the theoretical data presented in previous pages, it is difficult to employ intonation systems during performance, because then one's technique is applied "under pressure."

Commence with a G major scale, playing and analyzing simultaneously:

Exer. 85

Looking away from the music, repeat this exercise and visualize all of the notes and markings. Approximate the rhythmic notation.

Next, try to improvise a similar exercise in G harmonic minor. In measures 6 and 11 use the minor Subdominant harmony, whose E♭ is played ↓ .

Having retained all the marks mentally, transpose the exercises to A major and A minor--then B♭.

10.4 Analyzing chords from two given notes

Broken thirds are easier to analyze, because they contain two notes of each chord:

Exer. 86

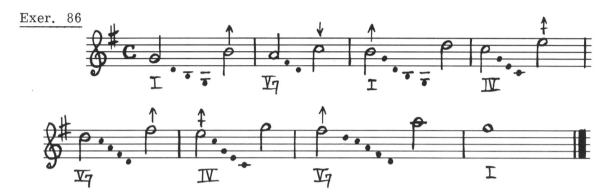

Do as you did before: play Exercise 86 in G minor, then in A and finally in Bb--both major and minor, descending as well as ascending. A passage such as

appears simple. Yet, we have occasionally heard such passages performed with faulty intonations. If the tunings of E, F, and B were not exaggerated, it would lead to disappointing results even after hours of practice.

Under analysis, a fast passage of broken thirds in C major is played as follows:

Exer. 87

F has a parenthesized arrow should that note be the seventh of the V. Lift the second finger quickly to allow room for the first finger.

In Eb major, lift the fourth finger to make room for the sharpened third finger:

Exer. 88

10.5 Gapped melodies

Continuing a previous discussion, the following aspect concerns those tones that are common to two harmonies. In Exercise 89, asterisks identify such situations. Indicate two Roman numerals under each asterisk as well as single Roman numerals beneath the other notes. Mark down the arrows or think of them mentally:

Exer. 89

In measures 1 to 3 of Exercise 89, "C" is either the Tonic's root or the Sub-dominant's fifth, both of which remain unaltered. The "F's" of bars 4 and 6 should be slightly flatted in case the harmony is V.

Using the former procedure, analyze a melody with larger-sized intervals:

Exer. 90

If you are convinced--in particular situations--that the harmony could only be IV, regulate the intonations accordingly. Usually, you will find it safer, however, to favor the V pull.

Apply your knowledge in G minor, relating every note to one or two chords:

Exer. 91

[Winds and singers proceed to Section 10.7.]

10.6   Acceleration

Refer back to Exercise 89.   Play it slowly once again, but use those exaggerated intonations that would sound excellent in fast tempos.   Even though plaguing to your neighbors' ears, repeat the exercise three or four times.   Don't hesitate to play

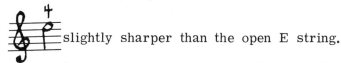 slightly sharper than the open E string.

Accelerate the speed gradually, and then play the following version:

Record it on tape, and listen, critically, to the play back.

Repeat the same procedure for Exercises 90 and 91.   Following are their fast versions:

If the above plan is carried out while practicing concertos and other violin literature, the intonation will be greatly improved.

10.7   Three harmonies in modulation; atonality

At this point, however, only three chords have been considered: I, IV, and V; other chords and aspects will be discussed later.   Some of these chords appear briefly in the études that follow.   The G of measure 5 in Etude 10 is ↓ , whereas the G of measure 10 is ↑ ; both cases conform to the rules of Chordal Intonation.   Modulations are scarce but important.

The melody of Etude 11 is slightly atonal, but--even so--intonation can be helped by using the Interval System and Chordal Intonation.

Etude 10

Allegretto

T. Podnos

Etude 11

Largo

T. Podnos

Chapter 11. GROUPS OF NOTES, PASSING NOTES, AND DOUBLE-STOPS

[Winds and singers may omit Sections 4 and 8 and Etudes 12 and 14.]

11.1   Reduction of tuning alterations

Your thorough analysis of each note has accomplished two things. First, like dissect-ing an insect under a microscope, you have analyzed intonation to find out "what makes it tick." In this manner, you have diagnosed the nucleus of many tuning problems. The second accomplishment concerns the reliability of the Chordal Intonation system. Problems that could not be solved by the Interval and Accidental Systems were solved by Chordal Intonation. Each of these systems provided solutions for many tuning problems. Did you notice, when applying them, that you used your mental skills? As a result of this procedure, have you noticed that your practice time was shortened?

No doubt, you have found the analysis of single notes--during performance of fast passages--to be extremely difficult. Consider the following aids. Groups of notes that include three-note arpeggios entail the adjustment of only one of those notes in each harmony. In the following exercise, merely alter the thirds as indicated; play the other notes with approximate piano tunings:

Exer. 95

These I and IV chords are supplemented occasionally with the notes A and D, respectively. Such added intervals of the sixth do not affect the aforementioned intona-tions of the basic triads; the thirds of the chords are still the most sensitive:

Exer. 96

89

In Exercise 81, page 76, twelve alterations were required when using the Interval System; if Chordal Intonation were used, only six alterations would have been necessary. In Exercise 96, use of the Interval System would require thirty-one computations, whereas only eight would be necessary using Chordal Intonation. The final score of 31 to 8 reaffirms the practicality of Chordal Intonation.

In preceding chapters, four-note chords of the I and IV harmonies received no discussion. They are featured here, however, because of their relationship to the present study concerning groups of notes. Other triads and four-note chords will be discussed later.

If you concentrate on the alterations of E, F, and B, the following passage becomes simple:

Exer. 97

Practice the same passage in minor and in other keys; continue concentrating on the third, fourth, and seventh degrees:

Exer. 98

11.2 Alternating between different systems

Use the Interval and Accidental Systems when playing the type of minor scale having two augmented seconds:

Exer. 99

Play Exercise 99 an octave higher, and note the new circumstances that occur.

Frequently, you will have to determine intonations by alternating between systems--all within a few bars:

Exer. 100

Liszt surprises musicians with similar writing.

In C major, arpeggios alternating with short scale-like figures involve two systems:

Exer. 101

Broken thirds are slightly complicated when they commence on weak beats, as in measures 3 and 4 of Exercise 102a. In Exercises 102b and c, semitone embellishments should always be minute; continue improvising the same sequences for two octaves, ascending and descending:

Exer. 102 (a)

(b)

(c)

There are, of course, many other types of passing notes and groups of notes that will become easier after analyzing them. You will find such figurations in Etudes 12 and 13 (pages 96 and 97), which follow the next discussion concerning double-stops.

Throughout the preceding text, intonations of altered notes were highlighted. You dovetailed those altered notes with unaltered notes that were tuned to piano ratios. While practicing fast music in D major, the third of the V--C♯--was rendered very sharp, whereas D had to maintain rigidity. This interplay between altered and unaltered notes occurs frequently. First there is tension, then there is rest; first suspense, then resolution. Similar situations have also prevailed in harmonic relationships of musical composition and were discussed at great length by Paul Hindemith. [2]

11.3   Double-stopped major scales for soloists and duets

Having incorporated altered and unaltered intonations in single melodic lines, we will now learn how to employ those forces in double-stopping. This information is also valuable to conductors when correcting group tunings. For their purposes, however, they will find more enlightenment in Chapter 18, which analyzes chamber music. Winds and singers may practice duets.

It is easy to realize that intonations of broken thirds can also be applied to double-stops. Following is a C major scale of broken thirds, which you practiced previously:

Compare the arrows with those in the following exercise; they are almost identical.

Exer. 103

One exception occurs on the last beat of the first measure. Both F and A, played simultaneously, comprise the two basic notes of the IV chord; A is, therefore, slightly sharpened. In the preceding example of broken thirds, F could be either the root of IV or the seventh degree of V--a situation that accounts for the parenthesized arrow. Reassure yourself, in either case, by playing F very close to the E which precedes it.

Now that you understand the theoretical aspects of double-stops, commence slowly when applying the rules. Major thirds are not difficult. On the first beat, the intonation of E is raised; thus, the interval C to E becomes enlarged.

[Winds and singers proceed to Section 11.5.]

11.4 Physiology for violinists

If you look carefully at your fingers in a mirror, you will notice that your first finger is now closer to the third finger than it would be if you played an E♭. Hence, a double-stopped major third is easier to play than a double-stopped minor third.

Some violinists find such minor thirds slightly difficult in the first position. When arriving at the second beat of Exercise 103, the second finger must be extended back to play the lowered F. This minor third becomes still more problematical when played with vibrato. Since great tension arises in this case, vibrato could help develop muscles of the hand. Such calisthenics will be discussed at the end of this chapter.

When shifting to ♪ in the third position, aim your third finger at your nose. Observe how you separated your fingers for this minor third. The first measure is completed with notes of the IV chord.

11.5 Small semitones

Analyze the second measure of Exercise 103, stressing small-sized semitones. Then play the entire exercise, both ascending and descending. Do not attempt to play it fast until you have mastered the intonations at a slow tempo!

D major and B♭ major come next:

Exer. 104

Exer. 105

Analyze other double-stopped major scales found in your favorite scale book.

11.6 Double-stopped broken thirds for soloists and duets

If you have already practiced double-stopped broken thirds, apply Chordal Intonation to them:

Exer. 106

Exer. 107

11.7 Double-stopped minor scales

Minor scales are slightly more complex because of their variable sixth and seventh degrees. Note the minor and major IV harmonies:

Exer. 108

The notes affixed with asterisks, below, belong to a chord that will be studied in Chapter 16. For the present, alter those notes according to the Interval System:

Exer. 109

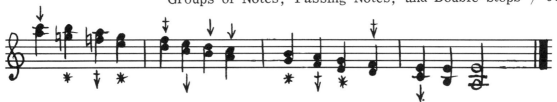

Alterations of sixths are accomplished by inverting all thirds; a major third, such as 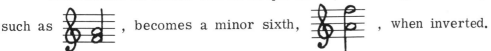 , becomes a minor sixth, , when inverted.

Working once again in A minor, a double-stopped scale of sixths includes the same arrows as the scale of thirds found in Exercise 109. Use the Interval System for notes with asterisks:

Exer. 110

Minor structures containing augmented seconds present additional problems:

Exer. 111

The following études feature passing notes, groups of notes, double-stops, and other aspects. In Etude 13, use the awkward fingerings as indicated.

[Wind or voice duets may practice the half- and quarter-notes of Etude 13: then proceed to Etude 15.]

11.8 The dependable Pythagoras

You may train yourself further in double-stops by analyzing and practicing two famous études: Jacob Dont's Opus 35, No. 8, and Rodolphe Kreutzer's No. 33. Substitute quarter-notes for Dont's sixteenth-notes. Note the "open string cases" and extension of fingers in the Kreutzer; supplement that étude with vibrato. On cold winter mornings, better circulation of the blood in the fingers can be induced by practicing the Kreutzer with a very wide vibrato for one or two minutes.

When playing the double-stops, alter the intonations according to Pythagoras' measurements.[3] Note the versatility of his tuning scheme; it is always dependable

Etude 12

Andante

T. Podnos

Etude 13

Etude 14

Allegro

Jacob Dont, Op. 35, No. 8

Etude 15

Andante

Rodolphe Kreutzer, No. 33

and is practical in any key. By analyzing the different keys in both études and the double-stops in the Kreutzer, you will train yourself to perform with better intonation in duets and quartets (as well as in larger ensembles).

Further discussions concerning modulation will be featured in the following chapter.

NOTES

1. See the abbreviation list at the beginning of this book.

2. Paul Hindemith, The Craft of Musical Composition, Book I (Mainz, 1937); translated by Arthur Mendel (London, 1942), pp. 115-121.

3. When we turn on electric lights or appliances at home, we occasionally think of Thomas A. Edison, who made such conveniences possible. In a similar sense, Pythagoras could be revered for providing us with a scheme, basic to good intonation.

Chapter 12. MODULATION

_____

[Winds and singers may omit Sections 2 and 4.]

12.1 The importance of the Dominant chord

Many works remain in one key for long periods of time, while other works constantly
fluctuate between tonalities. When changing keys, you usually find chords which help
the modulation. Of all such chords, the Dominant is the most common.

Kreutzer's Etude No. 2 features the Dominant-chord type of modulation several
times. In Exercise 112, repeated sequences are omitted, and V chord harmonies are
written out:

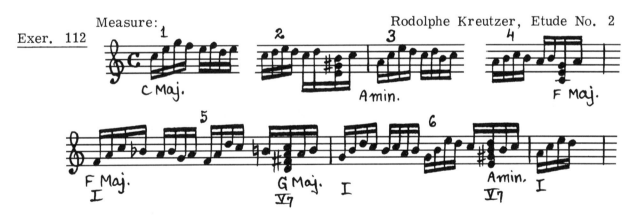

Braunschweig: Litolff, No. 507, [n.d.].

The modulation to A minor in measure 2 presents no problem, because the
note B is the fifth of the V chord and requires no alteration. Likewise, the note G
of measure 4 is to be played without alteration. At the end of measure 5, however,
C should be lowered, since it is the seventh of the V chord. The same adjustment
holds true in measure 6, containing D--again the seventh of the V.

To digress from the subject of modulation: there are three measures (later in the same étude) which--although in C major--have always presented problems. While playing these, concentrate mostly on the uppermost notes, which are part of a C major scale. As for the other notes, remember to alter E, B, and F in particular:

Exer. 113

[Ibid.]

[Winds and singers proceed to Section 12.3.]

12.2 Graphic aids

Kreutzer's Etude 35 has modulations that are analyzed easily, because the chords are already notated. In measures 11 to 16 of this étude, be sure to differentiate between lowered third degrees of minor keys and raised thirds of major keys. Analyze all the chords:

Exer. 114

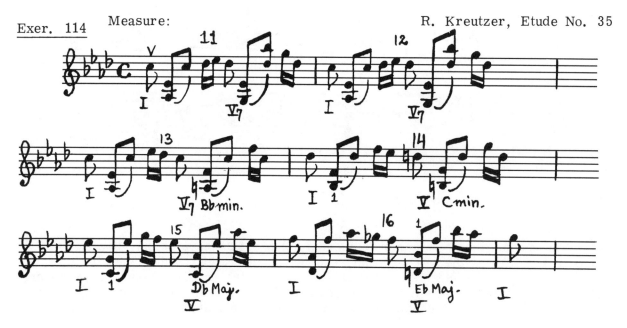

[Ibid.]

When accidentals are added after the initial statement of harmony, they sometimes indicate that the music is progressing to a new key. First, you see the accidentals, an act that relays a message to your brain to prepare for a new tonality. In measure 13 you encountered an A♮, in measure 14 a D♮ and B♮, and in measure 16 a D♮.

Many accidentals occur, however, after you arrive in the new key. This condition existed when modulating to D♭ major in measure 15; the G♭ of this key was not included until measure 16.

Of course, there are innumerable types of modulations, which, if discussed in detail, would require many pages--far too extensive for this study. As an aid, depend upon the Accidental System to alert you to these, and then use Chordal Intonation when altering particular notes of chords.

12.3   Practicing with printed chords

Jacob Dont's Etudes and Caprices, Opus 35, contains many modulations for analysis and practice. Dont's first étude includes a few new chords, such as the diminished seventh, which occurs in measures 18, 22, 42, and 46. That chord, as well as other new ones, will be discussed in forthcoming chapters.

Violinists may practice Etude 16 (Dont's No. 1) four different ways:

1. Soprano part
2. Soprano and Alto, simultaneously
3. Bottom part
4. All parts as written

Winds and singers may practice individual voices, all the while analyzing the chords in advance. Then two parts may be used as a duet, followed by three parts for a trio.

[Winds and singers proceed to Chapter 13.]

12.4   How to practice duets

You may have used what you learned thus far when playing duets: possibly in quartet playing also. Did you notice how essential good intonation is in Classical music?

On page 106 is Two-part Invention (Etude 17) presented in score form. First, practice each part separately. Then play each part in unison with another violinist who has also been studying this method; that would be a practical way for both of you to test your tunings. Next, alternate the parts with each other.

Version I includes arrows for practice purposes; Version II omits the arrows for performance--encouraging you to use your memory. When playing triplets, look for diminished fifths and augmented fourths, particularly when they span two intervals, melodically:

Etude 16

Prélude

Jacob Dont, Op. 35, No. 1

In Classical and Romantic works, the presence of those intervals frequently indicates Dominant (V) or Supertonic (II) harmonies (see Chapter 14). Etude 17 has many V$_7$ harmonies containing diminished fifths and augmented fourths.

Etude 18 (Dont's No. 3) has a great variety of tonalities from bar 11 to bar 22. Study the second and third beats of those bars in the following manner:

Exer. 115

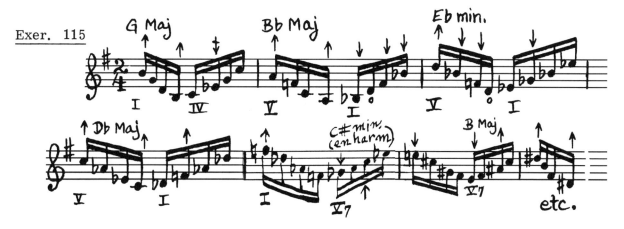

Then practice the entire section as originally written.

Etude 17

Moderato · Two-Part Invention · T. Podnos
Version I (For Study)

Etude 17

Moderato

Two-Part Invention
Version II (For Performance)

T. Podnos

Etude 18

Jacob Dont, Op. 35, No. 3

Measure 22

restez a la position. _ _ _ _ _ *restez* _ _ _

THE SUBORDINATE CHORDS

Chapter 13.   THE DIMINISHED SEVENTH CHORD

___

[Winds and singers may omit Section 3.]

13.1   Derivation from basic harmonies

All three primary chords discussed thus far comprise a basic study of Chordal Intonation.   There are many other chords, however, that derive from the I, IV, and V, and it is those subordinate chords upon which attention will be focused in this section.

The diminished seventh chord (VII$_o$)--built on the seventh degree of a scale-- has four notes, all of which are spaced a minor third apart.   Thus, in C major, you will easily recognize the VII$_o$ in its root position:

___

Ex. 19

___

The three inversions of that chord contain augmented seconds:

___

Ex. 20

___

Primarily, this subordinate chord derives from the V, whose fundamental note in C major is G:

112

Ex. 21

You could actually call this a V_7 chord with a flatted ninth added.

13.2   Enlargement of augmented seconds

First, remember that equal temperament--with its tuning compromises--makes no distinction between minor thirds and augmented seconds. If musicians try to use equal temperament, it is very difficult and sometimes results in false intonations. Good intonation can be guaranteed if one follows the rules of the Interval System and enlarges the augmented seconds. In Example 20, lower A♭ and raise B♮.

Using those alterations, the notes of the VII_o resolve to the I chord in a natural manner. A♭ gravitates toward G, and B gravitates towards C:

Ex. 22

Furthermore, a fast passage, such as

will always sound in tune when played with the above alterations.

You can also apply these rules when playing the octave passages at the end of the first page in Mendelssohn's Concerto. Here, the augmented second, B♭-C♯, must be spread apart to produce good intonation.

In Etude 19, the VII_o is featured as part of different chord progressions (I-VII_o-I, V_7-VII_o-I, V_7-VII_o-V_7), thus revealing its versatility.

Etude 19

Moderato

T. Podnos

Winds and singers may solve breathing problems by omitting the last notes of even-numbered measures.

[Winds and singers may study Etude 19, then proceed to Section 13.4.]

13.3 Thirty intonations to the octave

Many compositions contain enharmonicism in adjacent measures. As a result, we will occasionally see a passage such as:

 Ex. 23

The tempo, marked "Moderato," infers that we should play F♯ and G♭ with very slight alterations. Contrarily, if the tempo were marked Presto and the notes were printed with sixteenth values, we naturally would raise F♯ and lower G♭ to a greater degree (see Chapter 17). Such alterations compare with those discussed initially in Exercise 31, page 26.

With regard to the extent of tuning alterations employed by performing violinists, consider the following data. Example 24 has three ranges: 1) E up to D♭ (C♯); 2) F up to E♭♭(D); and 3) F♯ up to E♭.

Ex. 24 Enharmonicism in Diminished Seventh Chords

When pianists play the twelve notes of number 1, you actually hear but four different sounds. E and F♭ sound identical on the piano, as do C♯ and D♭. The same characteristics hold true in numbers 2 and 3. To play Example 24, pianists press only twelve finger keys, ranging from E up to E♭. Violinists, on the other hand, use many tunings for the same twelve notes: actually, eighteen in slow tempos, and an additional twelve in fast tempos. In summation, the finest violinists, when playing Example 24 in both slow and fast speeds, use thirty intonations!

13.4 An avenue to fifteen keys

The VII$_o$ chord has been a boon to composers for centuries, because it contains characteristics that facilitate modulations to various keys. We undoubtedly realized this when first glancing at the various accidentals of number 1. By practicing the following étude--with its many key changes--we will become adept in a new technique. The key is D major, which features the VII$_o$ chord C♯, E, G, and B♭. Etude 20 adheres to that notation with the exception of bars 29 and 31; in those bars, C♯ is replaced with D♭ to match the D♭ of measure 30. Winds and singers may prefer a moderate tempo.

The following is a list of keys to which we will modulate after leaving the above VII$_o$ chord.

TABLE III Harmonic Resolutions of the Diminished Seventh Chord of D Major As Found in Etude 20.

Key	Measure	Key	Measure
B♭ Maj.	3	A min.	28
G Maj.	5	D♭ Maj.	30
F♯ (V)	7	D Maj. (V)	32
F min.	11	E♭ Maj.	34
E min.	13	B♭ Maj.	38
G Maj.	15	G Maj.	40
D min.	19	F♯ (V)	42
B Maj.	22	D Maj.	52
A♭ Maj.	24	D Maj.	54
A Maj.	26		

Etude 20

Allegretto

T. Podnos

Chapter 14. THE SUPERTONIC AND AUGMENTED SIXTH CHORDS

14.1 Altering two notes of a triad

Deriving from the IV, the Supertonic (II) triad is built on the second degree of the scale. Two of its three notes require tuning alterations. In G major, raise the E of the II just as you would raise that note when playing a IV arpeggio:

Ex. 25

In addition, raise the A so that it forms a perfect fifth with E.[1]

Exer. 116

The II derives from the IV in other ways. Since we would normally lower E♭, the third of the minor IV chord, we should also lower E♭ when it occurs in any of the varieties of the II. The following exercise features one of these varieties:

Exer. 117

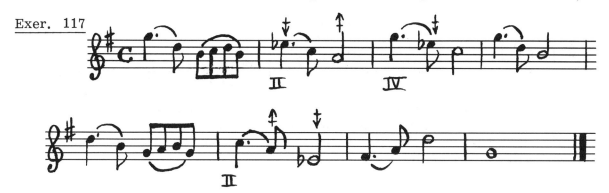

Next, we will use an A♭ in measures 2 and 6 of Exercise 117:

That II variety is known as "the Neapolitan sixth."

Exercise 96 of Chapter 11 featured a IV harmony supplemented by an extra note; such a four-note structure was really an inversion of the II₇ chord.

In the following exercise, practice the four types of II chords that have been discussed thus far. The group of sixteenth-notes in measure 6 contains a fifth type: the Supertonic seventh chord with a flatted fifth:

Exer. 118

14.2   The French and German sixth chords

Some composers write different II structures in succession, as in measures 2 and 3 of Exercise 119. Use the Accidental System in measure 6:

Exer. 119

What were those two beautiful harmonies in measure 6? They are called the French and German sixth, respectively, and are classified as chords of the augmented sixth. That interval occurs between the lowest and highest voices of those chords when they appear in the following position:

Ex. 26

Lower E♭ and raise C♯, the reason being that both of those notes are foreign to G major. Such alterations compare with similar ones already made in the Beethoven quartet (Exercise 41, page 33). If you recall, flatted notes usually resolve in a downward direction, whereas sharpened notes ascended; such a force was called "gravitation."

Example 27 also includes that intonational trait. Depicted below are the most common resolutions of the French and German sixth chords--to the I or V:

Ex. 27

Owing to the pull of both D's--soprano and bass--the augmented sixth, E♭-C♯, is greatly enlarged; it measures 1020 Cents according to Table II.[2]

What happens if E♭ is placed in the soprano? Such voicing produces the awkward descending interval E♭ to C♯. Pianists play it as a whole-tone, whereas violinists reduce its size to 180 Cents. If we examine Table II, we will see that 180 Cents is much smaller than the piano tuning.

14.3 Modulation through augmented sixth chords

Augmented sixth chords are regarded as chromatic, for they contain elements borrowed from other keys. As a result, those chords are suitable vehicles for modulation. In this sense, they are nearly as valuable as the VII° chord. Ask yourself two questions while analyzing augmented sixth chords: 1) "Is a modulation in progress?" 2) "If so, what is the modulation?" Composers--when writing the German 6th chord of G major,

for instance--occasionally replace C♯ with D♭, by which the German sixth becomes the V7 of A♭ major or minor. Some composers, however, neglect changing the C♯ to D♭. When that occurs, we ourselves must change the notation (mentally) as well as the tuning. [3] The aforementioned chord progression is but one among many possibilities by which composers modulate from augmented sixth chords to distant keys.

14.4 A new rule for the Accidental System

To comply with all of the above circumstances, the original rule of the Accidental System must now be lengthened: <u>Exaggerate intonations in the direction indicated by accidentals, particularly those accidentals derived from other keys.</u>

In Etude 21, <u>which is in C major</u>, try to locate each of the ten modulations containing augmented sixth chords. Do not be distracted by <u>appoggiaturas</u> (non-chordal tones), other modulations, or new harmonies. In the thirteenth and fourteenth measures from the end--an enharmonic case--use piano tunings for D♭ and F♯ so that they form a perfect fifth.

14.5 Warning signs

You noticed, perhaps, that the French sixth was voiced differently in the third and fifth bars; the third bar featured A♭ in the lowest register, whereas the fifth bar contained an F♯. While playing the étude, did you find it difficult to recognize augmented sixth chords because of the different voicings? It would have been much easier to identify those chords by looking for their enharmonic traits. Such conspicuous notations act as warning signs! In Etude 21, C major included F♯-A♭; in other compositions the key of A♭ major would feature D♮-F♭, while E major would contain A♯-C♮. These awkward intervals startle our eyes much more than the augmented seconds of VII° chords.

A psychological problem sometimes arises when playing augmented sixth chords. We agree to enlarge the augmented sixth interval but may hesitate to contract the enharmonic whole-tone. In examining measure 3,

Etude 21

Moderato   T. Podnos

cont'd.→

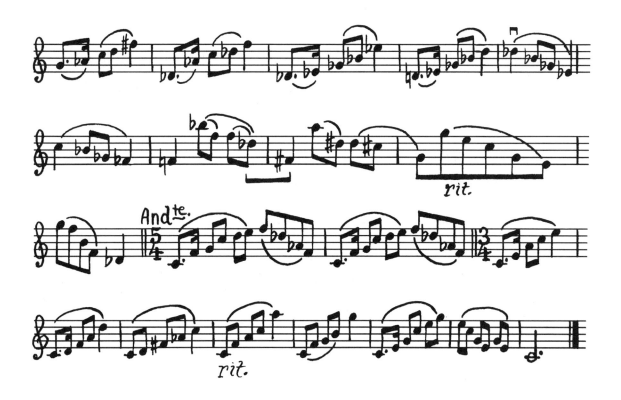

it becomes apparent that the upper A♭ must form a perfect octave with the lower A♭. Therefore, the size of F♯-A♭ must be reduced; such is the case in Pythagorean Intonation. If this brief explanation has provided further enlightenment, practice Etude 21 again.

Since you played in numerous keys (often passing through them quickly), and since new accidentals were often added, the Accidental System's extended ruling became quite useful. This rule is also practical when performing complex harmonic progressions and intricate varieties of the II chord.

14. 6 Discarding arrows with split stems

Four more II chords of C major are shown as follows:[4]

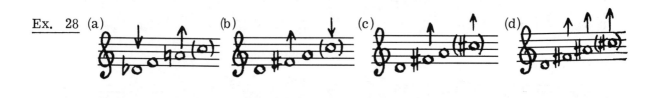

Some of those chords stray far from the C tonality and frequently contain modal traits. We could interpret other II harmonies as varieties of G major's V_7 chord:

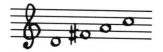

Exercises 120 and 121 include the arrows of Example 28, all of which have been notated without split stems. Parenthetic letters refer to the related harmonies in Example 28:

The augmented fifths are always spread apart.

Notice the effectiveness of the following II harmonies as mysterious background music:

Exer. 121

The composer or conductor will ask for crescendos and diminuendos, which, when coordinated with the above varieties of the II chord and your good intonation, will contribute toward the desired effect.

NOTES

1. Depending on the context of the music in other instances, you may then decide to simply lower the third of the II chord rather than raise the root and the fifth. Both types of alterations provide correct relations between the three notes of the II chord.

2. If you are mathematically minded and wish to calculate, proceed as follows. Write down the Cents value given in Table II for C♯ --114. To that figure add 1200 Cents, thus enabling you to place C♯ an octave higher in the soprano range; the total is 1314 Cents. E♭ is listed in Table II as 294 Cents. By subtracting 294 from 1314 you will arrive at the answer:　　　　measures 1020 Cents.

3. There is scientific evidence that Boston Symphony string players indulge in identical practices. See Charles Shackford, "Some Aspects of Perception," Journal of Music Theory, Part I (November 1961), p. 169; p. 172, Example 5, measure 23; p. 173, Example 6, measures 13 and 15; p. 175; p. 201.

4. From here on, plain arrows will always be used. Thus, arrows with split stems will be discarded for the sake of simplicity.

Chapter 15.   THE MEDIANT, TONIC SEVENTH, AND SUBMEDIANT CHORDS

[Winds and singers may omit Etude 22.]

15. 1   A tuning subordinate of two chords

The tunings of the Mediant (III) triad derive from two chords: the I and the V.   As already noted, the third and seventh degrees of a scale require special tunings; both of these sensitive notes are found in the III triad.   Because of its position--midway between the I and the V--the III chord is unique:

In Exercise 122, which follows, there are two types of III chords.   The type found in measure 10 derives from a modal scale:

Lower the G♮ and D♮ according to the Accidental System.   In measures 2 and 8, raise D♯ and G♯ according to either the Accidental System or Chordal Intonation:

Exer. 122

15.2 Limitations of the Accidental System

Note that the E major signature of Exercise 122 contains sharps that coincide with the third and seventh steps of the scale.   This trait is also found in all other sharp keys, except G major:

On the contrary, signatures with flats never include accidentals for the third and seventh steps:

This then means that the Accidental System can be used in Example 29 but not in Example 30.   Thus, it is evident (once again) that knowledge of the varied systems helps to solve different problems of intonation.

The two Mediant chords studied in Exercise 122 also appear with an added seventh:

Ex. 31

The tuning of F♯ (the seventh) is unaltered, thus producing a perfect fifth with B.

Following are two other Mediant chords, whose tunings depend upon both the Accidental and Interval Systems:

Ex. 32

Flattened keys require different considerations. In the key of E♭, for instance, use Chordal Intonation for (a). For varieties b, c, and d, exaggerate all flats foreign to the tonality:

Ex. 33

By doing this, we arrive at the same alterations used in Examples 31 and 32.

In a discussion of seventh chords, we should particularly notice the perfectly tuned fifths in Example 31 and in Examples 33a and b.

We will also find perfectly tuned fifths in the Tonic seventh chord of E♭:

Ex. 34

Furthermore, the raised D forms a large-sized major seventh with E♭, the chord's root. Such tunings conform to the rules of the Interval System.

Practice Exercise 123, which is in a sharp key. In measure 5 note the new chord on the third beat:

Exercise 124 is identical to Exercise 123 except that it is in E♭ major. What problems exist in Exercise 124 that were absent in Exercise 123?

15.3 Derivation of the Submediant chord from the Tonic chord

The Submediant triad (VI), a subordinate of the I, is built on the sixth degree of the scale. In G major, raise B just as you would in the Tonic triad. Also, tune the E either a perfect fifth below B or a perfect fourth above it:

Exer. 125

The first measure of Exercise 125 contains all three notes of the I harmony and thus prepares the intonation for B in the second measure. That does not always happen. In measures 1 and 3 of Exercise 126, for instance, we must determine independently the correct tunings of the Submediant. [1] Measures 5 to 7, in G minor, contain a VI harmony whose root and fifth are lowered. Winds and singers may omit the final notes of even-numbered measures.

Exer. 126

We noticed, of course, that the fourth finger was required when playing E♮.

Composers occasionally add a seventh to the above chords. They also add the seventh to other VI varieties:

Ex. 35

Alter the intonations according to the Accidental System.

When studying the subordinate triads--VII, II, III, and VI--we learned that their tunings were directly related to the tunings of the three primary chords. Indeed, the harmonic and tuning affinities between primary and subordinate chords are as important to good intonation as gravitational force (already discussed in Chapter 3). The primary chords provide a harmonic foundation. The subordinate chords supply different colorings. Good intonation guarantees convincing tonality. Each of these elements contributes to the overall performance.

The following étude includes enharmonicism, varied chordal progressions, and modulations. When many accidentals occur, one after the other, allow them to govern your intonation just as markings on trees would direct you along a hiking trail. Measure 15 should be played enharmonically as a G♯ major triad, including D♯ (E♭), which should be tuned to match the D♯ of the preceding measure. Practice this étude in Moderato and Allegro.

[Winds and singers proceed to Chapter 16.]

NOTE

1. Similar to the discussion in Chapter 14, footnote 1, you may elect (on other occasions) to lower the third of the chord rather than raise the root and the fifth.

Etude 22

Moderato

T. Podnos

Measure 15

rit.

Chapter 16. THE AUGMENTED FIFTH CHORD AND DOMINANT SEVENTH VARIETIES

[Winds and singers may omit Etude 23.]

16.1 The predominance of the augmented fifth over the major third

In preceding chapters, the augmented fifth interval occurred in particular varieties of subordinate chords, but those varieties were considered subsidiary. Quite the opposite, augmented fifths play prominant roles when featured in Tonic or Dominant harmonies. Such chords frequently appear in works by Debussy and other French composers. [1]

The arrows of the following exercise indicate that the augmented fifth must be raised. Notice that the major third of the I chord no longer has an arrow; rather, the G♯ --foreign to C major--is more important than E:

The V chord with an augmented fifth parallels the I♯5 in tunings. Remember to raise only the fifth:

Did you remember to lower the A♭ in measure 5 after raising the G♯ in the preceding measure? That alteration was justified by the continuous motion of the exercise.

16.2 Whole-tone scales

Both of the above augmented fifth chords derive from whole-tone scales. Thus, the V♯5 is associated with a whole-tone scale built on G:

Ex. 36

It has been said that such a scale should be divided equally; any other type of intonation would appear ridiculous. A whole-tone scale should be played with equal divisions, but the use of such measurements will not guarantee good intonation when playing the arpeggiated figures in Exercise 128. Therefore, use equal temperament for the whole-tone scale, but use the Accidental System for the related arpeggio. When you play Exercise 128 in a presto tempo, visualize the arrows as follows:

Exer. 129

Alternate between Exercises 128 and 129, and try to remember the arrows.

There are two varieties of the V_7 chord that are founded on the whole-tone scale. One has a raised fifth, the other a lowered fifth:

You may have already noticed the flatted fifth chord when it occurred in Etude 4 (one bar from the end) and in Etude 21 (eleven bars from the end).

16.3 Other types of Dominant chords

Two other V forms feature a major seventh. The first of these--Example 39--has the same tuning characteristics as the I_7: the third and seventh are raised. Example 40 has an upward sweep.

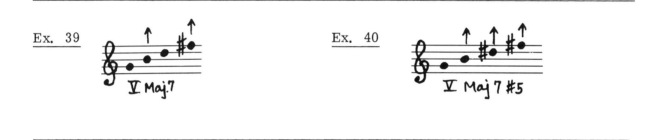

In Exercises 109 and 110, double-stopped minor scales in thirds and sixths contained notes affixed with asterisks. A suggestion was made to regulate the tunings of those notes according to the Interval System; now it becomes apparent that the harmony employed was that of the minor Dominant. When descending, the scale of A melodic minor included G♮--the third of the minor V:

Many composers supplement this triad with a seventh, which should be played a perfect fifth higher than the chord's third:

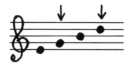

[Winds and singers proceed to Chapter 17.]

No doubt, we have heard other types of V chords, particularly those with added ninths, elevenths, and thirteenths. It is not necessary to discuss these in detail. In the following étude be sure to distinguish between large- and small-sized semitones.

NOTE

1. The augmented fifth chord is alleged to have been first used by Luca Marenzio (ca. 1560-1599). See William Pole, The Philosophy of Music (New York, 1924), p. 190.

Etude 23

Moderato

T. Podnos

grande rit.

Chapter 17.   ENHARMONICISM

[Winds and singers may omit Etude 24.]

17.1   Opposite tunings of C♯ and D♭

Enharmonicism, as explained earlier, is much less a problem to pianists than to
violinists; C♯ and D♭ sound identical on the piano.   Contrarily, violinists raise the
tuning of C♯ and lower D♭.   These practices began around 1800, at which time Campagnoli discarded Tartini's intonations and replaced them with Pythagorean. [1]   (See pp.
9-11.)

Tunings are more complex today than they were during Campagnoli's time.   In
Exercise 130, the tunings of G and C♯ (D♭) change according to the particular harmony.
Lower G and raise C♯ in the first bar; in the second bar--an opposite case--raise G
and lower D♭ (C♯). [2]

If you wish to compare the two sets of tunings more readily, play them in the
same register:

Consider the necessity for extreme exaggerations in fast performances, and notice
how the second and third fingers must constantly maneuver between the different tun-

ings.   Similar situations already occurred in Etudes 19 to 23, all of which required
quick thinking.   Exercises 130 and 131 are outstanding in that sense.

17.2   Adjusting inner voices in chamber music

Of course, if a string quartet were to play the above harmonies in stationary chords,
the first violinist would tune C♯ and D♭ identically, because both are in the melody.
The other players would have to alter their notes according to harmonic pull.   This
is the same technique we use for "open string" cases.

Ex. 41

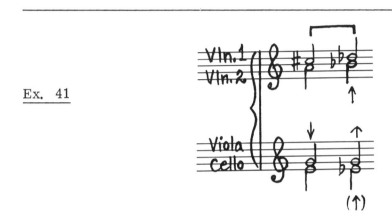

Because of the unusual alterations required in the second chord, the quartet may decide to try different tunings at rehearsals.   The tunings indicated in Example 41 should
be tried first.   Then the players should see if equal temperament provides better solutions.   If piano tunings are used, the first violinist will not raise the tuning of C♯,
nor will the violist lower the G in the first chord; such tunings should remain rigid
when progressing to the second chord.   It thus becomes apparent that equal temperament, a compromise tuning scheme, is quite valuable in slow, enharmonic progressions.

Examine Exercise 132, which follows, and note the enharmonic complexities
requiring various intonations.   In measure 1, G♯ is played high, whereas the A♭ of
measure 2 is played low.   The third measure's A♯ is high as contrasted to the fourth
measure's low B♭.   Playing in this manner, record these four measures on tape and,
when listening to the playback, notice how your ear readily accepts the different tunings.

Exer. 132   Moderato

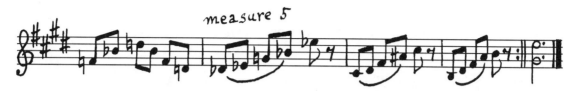

measure 5

If you play beyond the fourth measure, a different situation arises. Measure 5 contains a G, while measure 6 has an F♯. The other notes of these two measures are enharmonically identical (pianists would strike the same finger keys when playing D♭, E♭, and B♭ or C♯, D♯, and A♯). Since these sets of notes comprise the greater parts of measures 5 and 6, respectively, adhere to equal temperament throughout. Do not use Pythagorean intonation with its lowered flats and raised sharps, for, if you do, each measure will have a different pitch level.

17.3 Equal temperament in contemporary music

This chapter has alternated between discussions of slow and fast music. One reason for selecting such procedure concerns intonation problems found in performances of contemporary music. And, although it is not the intent of these writings to engage in lengthy analyses of atonal or avant-garde music, a few related aspects will be stated.

By rewriting Exercise 132 in chordal form (that is, vertically), the slow progressions will warrant tunings governed by equal temperament. Accordingly, the eight-measure score that follows is saturated with many enharmonic traits--too complex for the accidental or chordal systems. Use your knowledge of those systems and Tartini's tunings, however, and then compromise by using equal temperament.

Practice Exercise 133 four ways: 1) Study each voice separately. 2) Play the double-stops of the first line. 3) Next, play the double stops of line 2. 4) Finally, practice together with another violinist and alternate the lines. By doing this, both of you will train yourselves to play contemporary music with better intonation; this applies, of course, to those portions of contemporary compositions that feature slow-chordal progressions:

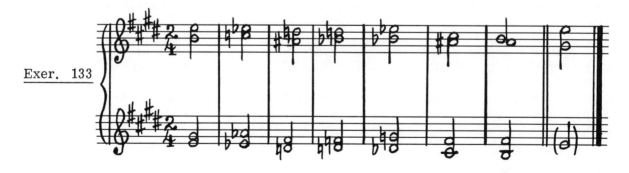

Exer. 133

Difficulties may be encountered when attempting to play with equal temperament, for we cannot measure intervals as accurately as a piano tuner. There are remedies, however, for these problems.

Consider three aspects in Examples 42 to 44, which follow. If your rendition contains intonations lying between those indicated and those of equal temperament, your playing will sound in tune. If you use equal temperament, the results will also be satisfactory. The third case--should you reverse the direction of the arrows--will contribute to false intonation. Use this knowledge at ensemble rehearsals, and then note your newfound ability to blend with other players. Moreover, when contending with a musician who habitually emits false intonations--either too sharp or too flat-- you will have foresight how to adjust your tunings, a technique that will improve the overall performance.

17.4 Common notes in different voices

In Exercise 133, you observed common notes in adjacent chords. Such common notes occur frequently in different voices. Examples 42 and 43 contain two different progressions that have proved problematic in ensemble work. Brackets point at notes common to both chords and indicate, further, that these notes should be performed with identical intonations.

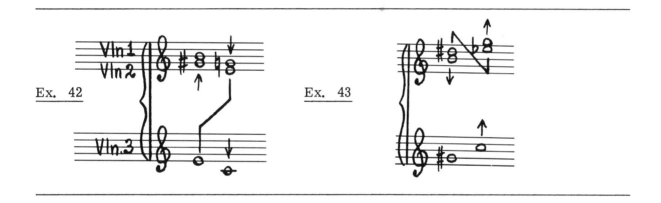

Ex. 42   Ex. 43

Example 44, in which the C minor chord appears first, is the reverse of Example 43.

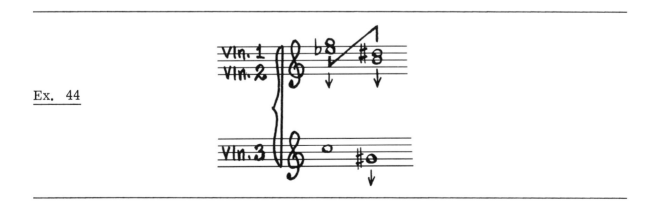

Ex. 44

While playing Examples 42 to 44, those musicians who strive to use equal temperament (all the while thinking also of Chordal Intonation) will arrive at a final product that will be fully satisfactory. As mentioned previously, such techniques prove invaluable when performing chamber music.

[Winds and singers proceed to Chapter 18.]

In the following étude, match the tunings of the enharmonic pairs of notes in the upper register: F♯-G♭, F♭-E♮, D♭-C♯, etc. Then alter the tunings of the other notes. The most practical notation is not always employed. Rather, you will find strange enharmonic relations, which, through practice, will enable you to play similar passages in other compositions. More exercise for your brain, precautionary accidentals--such as a natural for the fourth measure's E--are not included. Strive to play the étude without inserting such accidentals.

NOTES

1. David D. Boyden, The History of Violin Playing from Its Origins to 1761 (London, 1965), p. 371.

2. In his article "Some Aspects of Perception," Journal of Music Theory, Part II (April 1962), p. 68, Charles Shackford stated: "The important thing to music theory is the apparent reality of the difference between a diminished fifth and an augmented fourth...."

Etude 24

Lento

T. Podnos

Part IV

FURTHER ASPECTS OF PERFORMANCE

Chapter 18. CHAMBER MUSIC

18.1 General

Most scholars value the prefaces and introductions of books, because they explain the signs, methods, and other data in the text. But many lay-people all too often avoid these opening pages and thus miss important information. As a result, authors are often criticized unduly for omitting information in the main text that was already stated in the beginning pages.

18.2 Temporary and permanent solutions for problems

An analogy exists, perhaps, between that situation and this chapter. Seeking solutions for tuning problems at quartet rehearsals, some players will hastily consult this chapter. If they successfully locate the troublesome passages, they will also find arrows to help their intonation. This process, a temporary one, is not as beneficial as an understanding of the principles from which these arrows derive.

An examination of each passage should include analyses of intervals and accidentals (see Chapters 2, 3, and 13-17), as well as tempos to be played (Chapters 2-5, and 7). Good intonation in octave passages for two instruments results from application of those three aspects. Modulation and enharmonicism refer back to Chapters 12-14 and 17, while solutions for other tuning complexities are dispersed throughout the volume.

Quartet players occasionally solve tuning problems by rendering particular passages "a little on the sharp side" or "a little on the flat side." These players seldom realize why such procedures help intonation. If analyzed, it would become evident, perhaps, that such adjustments touched upon the characteristics of Chordal Intonation, the system that comprises the main study of this book. This system indicates how to plan an intonation before sounding it.

An arrow pointed upward suggests a raised tuning, whereas an arrow pointed downward suggests a lowered tuning. Arrows used when practicing individual parts can also be applied in quartet renditions.

When looking at quartet scores, many string players identify different chords easily. On the other hand, they experience difficulties in analyzing orchestral scores because of the transpositions for various wind instruments. Conductors are extremely adept at transposing, however, and will be able to solve tuning problems more quickly by marking arrows above certain notes in their scores.

18.3   Tuning falsities of perfect fifths

Nevertheless, it may surprise many conductors that perfect fifths need not be played too accurately when supplemented with other notes of a chord. Chapter 6 stresses that the major triad C, E, G should have an E tuned slightly sharp, whereas the minor triad C, E♭, G should have an E♭ tuned slightly flat. Such intonations are more important than the tunings of perfect fifths. When reporting laboratory analyses of perfect fifths performed by Boston Symphony string personnel, Charles Shackford stated: "The spread of ... a quarter tone between the largest and smallest fifths played is surprisingly large for the interval that is commonly supposed to be the most sensitive to inaccuracies of intonation."[1]   This information is equally valuable to quartet players and conductors.

18.4   Analyses of excerpts from seven string quartets

The above techniques should be applied when playing the multitude of ensemble works, which, unfortunately, cannot be analyzed in this short chapter. Of seven quartets selected, the following excerpts have been arrowed because of their intonation problems.

Both chamber players and conductors can benefit further by consulting Table IV after Chapter 19.

NOTE

1.   Charles Shackford, "Some Aspects of Perception," Journal of Music Theory, Part I (November, 1961), p. 185 (see also his pp. 186-188).

QUARTET I

If open A strings are used, lower all F's and C's in measures 1-4.　(See Exercise 50 and subsequent remarks.)

Movement I

Allegro spirituoso　　　　　　　　　　　　Joseph Haydn, Op. 74, No. 2

QUARTET II

If the open A string is used in measure 25, lower the preceding notes. (See Exercise 50.)

Movement I   Joseph Haydn, Op. 74, No. 3

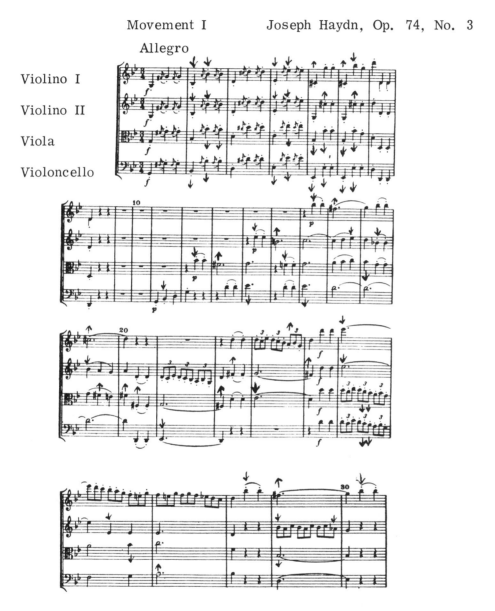

Edwin F. Kalmus, No. 202.

QUARTET III

Movement IV

Joseph Haydn, Op. 76, No. 1

Scarsdale, N.Y.: Edwin F. Kalmus, No. 203, [n.d.], pp. 20.
Used by permission of Belwin-Mills Publishing Corporation.

QUARTET IV

Movement II   Joseph Haydn, Op. 76, No. 4

From 1873 edition of Quartet XI, pp. 75-76.   Used by permission of C. F. Peters Corporation.

QUARTET IV (cont'd)

open string case.   (See Exercise 50 and
remarks.)

Ibid. , p. 76 (cont'd).

QUARTET V

Movement I   W. A. Mozart, K. 465

Adagio

Mozart Quartet VI in C Major.   Kassel: Bärenreiter, [n.d.], p. 145.
Used by permission of Music Associates of America.

QUARTET V (cont'd)

Allegro

Ibid. , p. 146.

QUARTET V (cont'd)

Ibid., p. 147.

QUARTET VI

Movement I　　　　　　　　　　　W. A. Mozart, K. 589

Allegro

Mozart String Quartet in B [♭]. Kassel: Bärenreiter [n.d.], p. 243.
Used by permission of Music Associates of America.

QUARTET VI (cont'd)

Ibid., p. 244.

QUARTET VI (cont'd)

Ibid., p. 245.

QUARTET VII

Ludwig van Beethoven, Op. 18, No. 1

Movement II

Adagio affettuoso ed appassionato

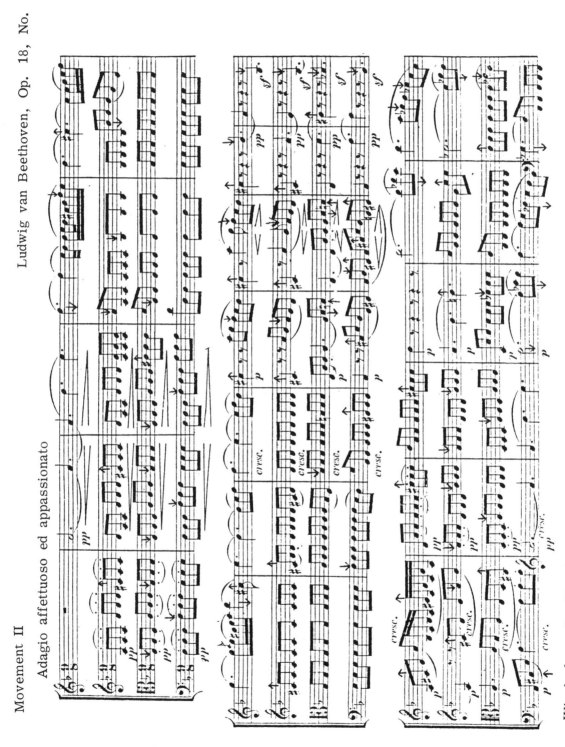

Wiesbaden: Breitkopf und Härtel p. 8.
Used by permission of G. Schirmer, Sole U.S. Agents.

Chapter 19. OTHER INTONATION PROBLEMS OF VIOLINISTS

19.1 General

Most of the practice material in this text is written in the first to third positions. By using that limited range, intonation traits are presented more clearly than they would be if the entire fingerboard were discussed. Perhaps you noticed that tuning principles applied in the lower positions also proved useful in other registers.

Now that you have solved certain problems, you may wish to know of others that also affect intonation.

19.2 Finger gauging

Directed toward younger violinists, the following techniques produce better intonation in the first five positions. First to be stressed is the term "the well-gauged hand." This term refers to our four fingers as they span the interval of a perfect fourth. A common example occurs in the first position:

Ex. 45
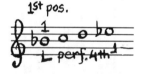

Those four fingers can also be used for playing similar phrases in any position. When playing Example 45 followed by a similar sequence in the fifth position,

---

Ex. 46
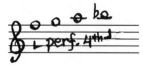

---

we must anticipate shifting all four fingers with great precision. After the hand arrives in the fifth position, it is necessary that the tuning measurements remain the same.

The term "well-gauged hand" has often been referred to as a "block." A still better term would be "wooden block." Try to sense the rigidity of such a block, and apply that feeling to your fingers when shifting positions. As the hand ascends into the upper positions, such a block gradually diminishes in size:

Ex. 47   The Gauging of the First and Fourth Fingers in Different Positions

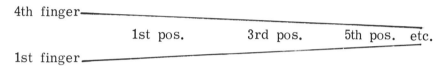

This fact is a technicality of physics that most students master with little difficulty. Great violinists continue to ensure their intonation by relying on the block. If you acquire utmost control of the block and retain the stability gained thereby, you will become more adept when playing in every position.

Exercise 134 contains artificial harmonics. When shifting from the first position to the fifth, note the variable distances between the first and fourth fingers:

The first finger is the most important, since it leads the way for the other fingers. Thus, when shifting with your fourth finger from E♭ up to B♭ (Example 48), hold down the first finger as well, and shift both fingers simultaneously (Example 49):

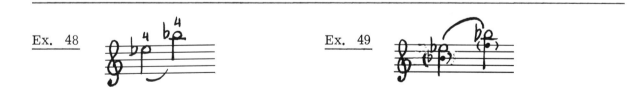

By making the block your bible, the intonation will improve when changing positions. You will acquire a feeling of security similar to that which you experience when standing on both of your feet; balancing yourself on only one foot produces instability. Of

course, the more you shift with the first and fourth fingers, the more precise your intonation will become. Eventually, you will be able to shift with only the fourth finger, while thinking of the first finger subconsciously.

19.3   Semitone extensions for small hands

Consider the different sizes of violinists' hands. If yours are normal or small, you will be able easily to lower the first finger a semitone or raise the fourth finger a semitone. Example 50 depicts the block, D to G, with its extensions, C♯ and G♯:

Ex. 50

In Example 50, abnormal stretching of the fingers is not required. That being the case, the use of semitone extensions is conducive to good intonation.

Play Exercise 135, and observe the practicality of the extended first finger, C♯ :

Exer. 135

Since you need not move the hand out of the third position, the block remains stable.

The same extension is found in other passages:

Exer. 136

Exer. 137

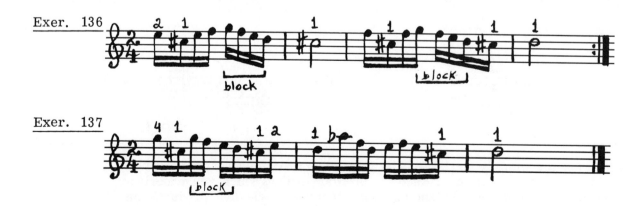

19.4 Whole-tone extensions for small hands

Next under discussion is an opposite case: an extension down to C♮. This stretch of a whole-tone contributes to false intonation when played by small or even normal-sized hands.

Exer. 138

Although fine for exercise work, whole-tone extensions are risky at performances.

Because of inherent characteristics of particular passages, there is sometimes no alternative but to engage whole-tone extensions; such instances do occur. But if those practices are indulged in constantly, the block, and thus the intonation, will be jeopardized.

Some violinists use whole-tone extensions in order to play phrases on only one string; thus they achieve a sound of uniform quality. If the intonation suffers, however, it would be better to use two strings, as indicated below:

Exer. 139

Thus, we see that uniform tone colorings are not as important to performances as playing "in tune."

19.5 Resonance

When we cross strings, better intonation is achieved as well as fuller resonance. In Example 51, note that C keeps sounding slightly longer than the printed note:

Ex. 51

This technique produces an overlapping of sounds similar to a piano with its loud (sustaining) pedal held down.   Bach achieved that effect in the "Preludio" of his E major Partita for solo violin:

Apply this two-string approach to other Bach works as well as to concertos, and notice how your playing takes on new character: resonant and brilliant.

19.6   Vibrato

Besides finer intonation and resonance gained by voiding whole-tone extensions, better vibrato is achieved.   Do you remember those early years of study when your teacher asked for vibrato on every note, even when practicing scales?   This contributed to beauty.   Continue that practice by discarding such fingerings as found in Exercise 140, for they restrict the hand.

Playing the first six notes on only the A string provides one tone color, and the stretch is not too difficult.   But did the note G have vibrato?   That note certainly requires vibrato, since it occurs on the downbeat.   Indeed, all downbeats should be played with vibrato, a practice that provides pulse to a composition.   To attain artistry, playing with proper pulse is a necessity.

The first measure of Exercise 140 contains a D whose half-note value encourages vibrato.   If we stretch for the G, the taut extension restrains the hand as if it were anchored.   True, we could vibrate on the G by concentrating, but in doing so, the hand's muscles would be over-exerted.   Burdened with this hardship--in addition to other performing problems--our minds may have been too occupied to think about vibrating on whole-tone extensions.   The results: dead notes.   We can now acquire finer intonation and vibrato by crossing strings or shifting positions, the next subject.

19.7   Shifting aided by inertia

As already mentioned, the hand and its fingers move together as a block when shifting positions; also the span of the first and fourth fingers diminishes gradually as the hand ascends the fingerboard.   As a result, such semitones as E-F or B-C are placed closer together in the higher positions than in the first position.

Moving from one position to another, however, entails more than different gaugings of the fingers.   Shift your hand four or five positions and observe what happens.   You commence by moving your hand, which then continues to travel until stopped. Scientists call that force inertia.   Inertia occurs every time you shift positions--ascending or descending.   When practicing fast works, note that shifting two or three positions is easier than shifting one; inertia helps to speed your hand great distances.   Therefore, to obtain better intonation in faster tempos, shift at least two positions.

In slower speeds, when inertia is almost dormant, it is appropriate to use one-position shifts.   This technique has been utilized by Heifetz, whose playing often features a descending slide of a whole-tone accomplished with one finger.   Such a device produces a beautiful effect.

19. 8   Whole-tone scales

There are blocks other than the perfect fourth already described.   When playing whole-tone scales, one usually fingers the block of an augmented fourth as follows:

Exer. 141

The first finger--which leads the block--ascends a half-position every four notes.

A different solution is employed by mandolinists, who descend a half-position every three notes:

Exer. 142

This fingering is presented here, because some violinists are unacquainted with it. Both of the above blocks are played readily by any sized hand.

19. 9   Muscle tension

That facet of the subject of blocks provides reason to mention one aspect of cello performance that, as you will soon see, relates to similar situations in violin playing. When playing in the higher positions, cellists frequently engage the thumb and the first three fingers; the fourth finger is used but occasionally. If the thumb touches the side of the instrument's neck in the middle positions, the fourth finger never

plays beyond [music notation] , whereas the third finger can readily play [music notation] . All of

those fingerings are executed easily. They are governed by the circular motion of the hand--right to left--which occurs while ascending the fingerboard.

    Violinists often finger passages strangely in order to solve particular problems. Sometimes they have to contend with bowing intracacies, or the phrase perhaps allows for a fingering less strenuous to the hand and finger muscles. Indeed, any fingering has merit that reduces the workload while promoting better intonation. One such example is found in the following extension of a perfect fourth:

Ex. 53

Other extensions in the upper positions are easier for long fingers than for short. In those high registers, violinists should use fingerings best adapted to their own hand.

19.10 Finger strengthening

Finger strain when playing double-stopped scales has already been realized. In violin methods of the past, numerous exercises were provided to limber--and thus strengthen --the fingers; the most famous of these stemmed from the teachings of Demetrius C. Dounis.[1] Many other violinists have devised their own setting-up exercises, such as the particular way of practicing Kreutzer's Etude No. 33 suggested in Chapter 11. Quite innovative, a certain Frank Macdonald (fl. 1920-1938) of Boston, who was an excellent violinist, concocted a machine to solve his problems. He inserted the fingers of his left hand into the machine and then turned a crank with his right hand. This was followed by immersing the left hand in hot water. Macdonald repeated that procedure a few times, after which he claimed he could execute double-stopped passages with great ease. An additional note: his intonation was excellent.[2]

    If you tone up the muscles of your fingers, they will respond more quickly when your mind requests sharp or flat tunings.

19.11 Fingerings that help intonation

To continue the discussion concerning fingerings: two measures from the Sibelius Concerto are analyzed:

Exer. 143   Jean Sibelius, Op. 47

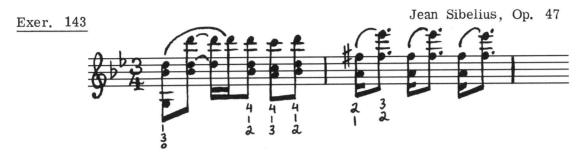

Berlin: Schlesinger'sche Buch- und Musikhandlung, Rob. Lienau, 1905.

In the first two chords, the block is well established. The second chord, however, contains a third finger played low and a fourth finger played a major tenth higher--a combination that creates tension. Contend with that fingering temporarily in order to set the block. The next time the same chord appears, alleviate the tension by playing B♭ with the second finger. Immediately, a relaxed feeling is experienced; the tightness of the third finger disappears. When possible, avoid pain to achieve better intonation.

If the said note were B♮, the third finger would have felt perfectly at ease. But not so with B♭.

The last beat of the measure contains an A played with the third finger:

A relaxed feeling is present. That sensation should be realized also on the last eighth-value of the bar when a former chord again appears; in that instance, you can relax your muscles by using the second finger for B♭, as you originally did.

Regardless of criticism, the fact that your intonation improves almost immediately confirms the practicality of such fingerings. The most valuable asset is not theory, but results.

The second measure of the Sibelius passage features a diminished seventh chord lacking a C. Here, the first three fingers are engaged in a natural manner. In other works, either that fingering or the combination 2, 3, 4 provides a tidy block.

19.12   Semitones in the ninth position

Retrogressing to single notes in fast tempos--but in the high treble range--the exaggerated tunings you have already studied become, indeed, an asset. A composition known by all advanced violinists, Sarasate's _Zigeunerweisen_, includes a passage often played "out of tune":

Exer. 144

Pablo de Sarasate, Op. 20, No. 1

(sempre 8va)

Of course, the fingers are quite cramped in such a high register. But, even when confronted with that problem, it certainly is possible to play "in tune" with the help of Chordal Intonation. Consider three aspects: speed; the Tonic chord's minor third (C); and the Dominant chord's leading tone (G#). Since the tempo is extremely fast, intonations must be extremely exaggerated. Many violinists emit C♮'s that sound like C#'s, even though unintentional. Possibly, they practiced the passage slowly without realizing that speed requires its own tunings. Those violinists sometimes blundered on six of the C's.

If vibration-per-second readings of the intended C♮'s were taken, you would perhaps find that those notes were slightly sharp. Quite the opposite, the key of A minor requires lowered C♮'s. A second reason for playing a low C♮ relates to the gravitation theory. C♮ is attracted to B; when positioned far away from B, C♮ sounds false. A third reason relates to the melodic circle:

Ex. 54

C♮ is on the outside of that circle, and thus the note becomes conspicuous to the ear. The tuning falsity is just as outstanding as a tall tree in a garden.

19.13 Rejection of false tunings in Western culture

When the artist finishes playing Zigeunerweisen, the audience applauds in recognition of the technical feats. But the listeners also retain the false intonation if such occurred near the end of the composition.

Hillbilly fiddlers often play C♮ with a sharpened intonation in the key of A minor. Musicologists call that tuning "neutral," since the sound falls half way between C♮ and C♯. In performances of much of the world's folk music, neutral tunings are common.[3] But in Western culture, such tunings are not customary.

Tartini's tunings were rectified by Campagnoli, and the author--by supplementing these principles--has ventured farther.

It is hoped that this volume will benefit its readers and that good intonation will result.

NOTES

1. Demetrius C. Dounis, The Absolute Independence of the Fingers in Violin Playing on a Scientific Basis, Op. 15 (London, 1924-26).

2. Working in the same field, Henry Ostrovsky (1875-1956), a violin pedagogue, invented machines for stretching and strengthening the hands. In a letter of October 19, 1976, his nephew, Fredy Ostrovsky of the Boston Symphony Orchestra, stated that--because of their therapeutic value--these machines also found their way into several Philadelphia hospitals, where their use has continued until the present day.

3. Theodor H. Podnos, Bagpipes and Tunings (Detroit, 1974), pp. 35-37.

Appendix I. TARTINI INTONATIONS

Tartini instructed his pupils to listen for sounds other than those produced by their fingers. To achieve this, his pupils proceeded as follows. First, they played a double-stop, such as 🎼. Next, the size of this major third was altered while one listened for another sound, D, two octaves lower in pitch. It was difficult to hear the resulting D, 🎼 , because its volume was very faint.

There is a way, however, to increase this volume. Obtain a small empty bottle approximately two inches high, having a square base (something equivalent to an iodine bottle). Holding an inexpensive violin under your chin, make certain that the G and E strings are the same distance from the floor. To do this, bend the uppermost part of your torso to the left, an uncomfortable position. Now, place the upright bottle on the belly of the violin, and position it next to the left side of the tailpiece. Take care not to allow the bottle to fall and scratch the violin.

While playing many varieties of double-stops, the bottle will bounce around slightly, causing a rattling sound. But, of greater importance, you will also hear the following resultant tones:

Ex. 55

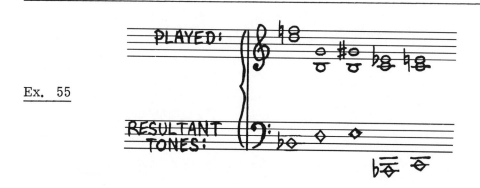

Physicists and musicologists have called these resultant tones "difference tones"; the vibrations-per-second readings of the alto voice, when subtracted from those of the soprano, equal the readings of the bass note, whose sound the bottle amplified.   However, if you use an expensive violin, no bottle is necessary to hear these <u>terzi tuoni</u> (third tones), as Tartini called them.

All Tartini thirds and sixths differ from equal temperament.   Major thirds and sixths are smaller than our piano's, whereas minor thirds and sixths are larger.

To find how the major third differs, for example, place your third finger on the A string (D, in the first position).   Match the tuning of your third finger with the same D of the piano.   Then, by using the bottle-method, find the F♯ on the E string, which when played simultaneously with the note D, will produce the resultant "third tone," D, in the bass.   If you compare your

to that of the piano, you will notice that your F♯ is slightly flat.

Ex. 56

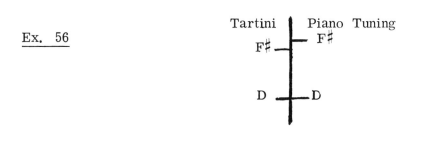

Throughout the centuries, many artists and scientists endorsed Tartini's "just intonation" with its resultant tones.[1]   Among these were Leopold Mozart, who wrote a book[2] in 1756 (revised 1770), and Hermann L. F. von Helmholtz, the world-famed musicologist, whose book appeared in 1863; he influenced his dear friend Joseph Joachim (1831-1907).   In 1937, Paul Hindemith endorsed and discussed combination and resultant tones on pages 58 to 68 of his first book.   All of these important people had great influence upon the musical world.

During our century, however, it was noticed that many musicians and singers who believed in Tartini intonations theoretically, used them but occasionally during performance.   This situation prompted laboratory tests, several of which have been discussed in Chapter 5.   One experiment, not discussed, occurred at the University of Washington.[3]   Here, 753 students performed 44 intervals in a space a little larger than a fifth.   The tests, conducted in a most scientific manner, revealed that the students had "no preference for the just [Tartini] major 3rd."   While making this observation, James Murray Barbour, the famous acoustical musicologist, added, "These experiments prove conclusively that Helmholtz and his followers are wrong, that singers have no predilection for the so-called natural or just [Tartini] intervals.... Neither singers nor violinists use just intonation."[4]

This fact is confirmed further in Leopold Auer's writings presented in my Chapter 1, the charts in Chapters 1 and 6, and the laboratory tests discussed in Chapter 5.

NOTES

1. Other resultant tones--faint and soprano--occur also, but these bear the name "combination tones." Georg Andreas Sorge, a German organist and theorist, discussed these in a composition book, Vorgemach der musikalischen Komposition (published 1745-1747), which preceded Tartini's 1754 publication by nine years. Still, Tartini's name is used throughout this text, since he was the first to discover "third tones," in 1714. See Grove's Dictionary of Music and Musicians, 5th ed., Vol. VII (London, 1954), p. 972; Waldo Pratt, ed., The New Encyclopedia of Music and Musicians (New York, 1929), p. 764; and Willi Apel, Harvard Dictionary of Music, 2nd ed., (Cambridge, 1972), pp. 185-186.

2. Leopold Mozart, Versuch einer gründlichen Violinschule (Augsburg, 1756); English translation by Editha Krocker (London, 1948). See her page 70.

3. E. R. Guthrie and H. Morrill, "Fusion of Non-Musical Intervals," American Journal of Psychology XXXIX (1928).

4. James Murray Barbour, "Just Intonation Confuted," Music and Letters, XIX (January 1938), pp. 48, 53.

Appendix II. AIDS FOR SINGERS AND WINDS

For more than a century, many singers and wind players emulated piano tunings, but benefited only partially from such practices.

In the following procedure, the author, while negating piano tunings, does use them as a basis from which to deviate. Performers will learn how to transform water-filled drinking glasses into a musical instrument having those intonations used by great artists. Only diatonic music will be discussed.

A small laboratory will take two hours to set up, and, in starting, you will need a piano, a table, a quart pitcher of water, a teaspoon, a comb, and four large drinking glasses (each approximately six inches high). If such glasses are not available, 32-ounce mayonnaise or salad-dressing jars may be used after removing their labels; do save the lids.

Assuming that the four glasses are accessible, we will obtain a different sound from each one. First, place a table near your piano. Then, place the glasses on the table, positioning them side by side, left to right. Fill glass number 1 completely with water. Tap the glass with a comb to hear if the glass's pitch matches a piano note. If the glass's pitch is sharper than the piano's, remove a little water with a teaspoon.

Next, fill glass number 4 approximately half way, seeking a perfect fourth above the first glass's pitch. Match the piano tuning by regulating the water level.

The scale's root and fourth have been completed. Now, the major second and third will receive delicate adjustment, because their tunings will differ from equal temperament.

Fill glass number 2 with less water than glass number 1 so that glass 2 sounds a whole-tone higher than glass 1. Match the piano tuning, then remove one teaspoon of water.

For glass 3, lower the water level further, all the while tapping the glass and listening for the scale's major third. Match the piano pitch. Follow up by removing three teaspoonsful of water.

179

The result will be the second step of a major scale tuned slightly sharper than the piano, and the third step tuned much sharper. Leading brass players endorse such thirds in Section 2.4. Because of such alterations, the semitone size between the major third and the fourth automatically becomes quite small.

These types of tunings will help our intonations while practicing. Play the said four notes on the piano; then tap them out on the glasses, and note the different intonations. Skip over certain glasses while you tap out broken thirds and various musical phrases; then play or sing the glasses' intonations. Use either different fingerings or muscle control (humoring) if necessary.

When retaining the water-filled glasses for future use, cover them with cardboard, small books, or plastic wrap to prevent evaporation; if you decide to use jars, their screw-on lids will protect the water level. To really retain the intonations at which you worked so diligently, record them with a cassette recorder. Remember to tap out different melodic structures to gain extra material. It would also be valuable to strike each glass several times, thus extending the sound a few seconds.

To complete the octave scale, use a second set of glasses about four and a half inches high.[1] Tune glasses 5 and 8 to piano pitches, sharpen 6 slightly (as you did number 2) and sharpen 7 very much (as you did number 3). After tapping out simple melodies, such as "Old Folks at Home," "Home Sweet Home," "Jingle Bells," and "Joy to the World," memorize the glasses' intonations before singing or playing them. Vocalists may wish to compare directly by singing and tapping at the same time.

A third set of glasses, approximately three and a half inches high, will provide an extra half-octave. Tune number 9 glass to 2, 10 to 3, 11 to 4, and 12 to 5. Now you are matching octaves as piano tuners do. This extended range may prove useful to singers with "low" or "high" voices. Wind instruments often have false intonations dispersed throughout their entire compasses. And then, many melodies have wide ranges.

If we wish to include two more glasses for the minor thirds, they will occur in sets one and three and should be tuned flat.

All of our glasses are now tuned and are ready to be recorded. As already mentioned, it is practical to tap each glass a few times to prolong the sound. If wind players listen to the cassette recorder's playback, they will hear it objectively, and their hands will be free to try different fingerings. It no longer will be necessary to pick up the comb and then tap the glasses.

Singers, also, will find it much easier to press a button and then have ten minutes of good intonation to match. The cassette recorder, which is light enough to be carried away from home, eliminates the water-evaporation problem and should prove to be a handy aide.

[Proceed to Section 2.4.]

NOTE

1. Glasses and jars are made of different thicknesses and densities, a condition that necessitates experimentation to find each vessel's sounding range.

TABLE IV

The Intonation of Sixty-three Chords in C Major and Minor

— means "Piano Standard"

	C	C#	Db	D	(D#) Eb	E	F	F#	G	(G#) Ab	A	(A#) Bb	B
I ♭3(7)	—				↓				—				↑
I ♮3(7)	—					↑			—				↑
I #5(7)	—					—				G#↑			↑
II (7)	—			↑			—				↑		
II ♭1 ♭5(7)	—		↓				—			↓			
II ♭5(7)	—			↑			—			↓			
II ♭1(7)	—		↓				—				↑		
II #3(7)	↓			—				↑			—		
II #3 ♭5(7)	—			—				↑		↓			
II #3(#7)		↑		—				↑			—		
II#3#5(#7)		↑		—				↑				A#↑	
III (7)				—		↑			—				↑
III ♭1 ♭5(7)				—	↓				—			↓	
III ♭1(7)				—	↓				—				↑
III ♭5(7)				—		↑			—			↓	

1

1. See Chapter 14, footnote 1, for other tunings.

TABLE IV (cont'd)

	C	C#	Db	D	(D#) Eb	E	F	F#	G	(G#) Ab	A	(A#) Bb	B
IV (7)	—				↑	—					↑		
IV b3(7)	—				↑	—				↓			
IV#1 b3	—							↑		↓			
IV#1 b3 b7	—			↓				↑		↓			
V (7)				—			↓		—				↑
V #7				—				↑	—				↑
V b5(7)		↓					↓		—				—
V #5(7)					D# ↑		↓		—				—
V b3(7)				—			↓		—			↓	
V b3(#7)				—				↑	—			↓	
V b3 b5 (7)		↓					↓		—			↓	
VI (7)	—					↑			—		↑		
VI b5(7)	—				↓				—		↑		
VI b1 b5(7)	—				↓				—	↓			
VI b1(7)	—					↑			—	↓			
VII (7)				—			↓				—		↑
VII b1(7)				—			↓				—	↓	
VII b1 b7				—			↓			↓		↓	
exception VII b1 b5 b7				—		Fb —				↑		↓	
VII b7				—			↓			↓			↑

2

2. See Chapter 15, footnote 1, for other tunings.

REFERENCES CITED

Apel, Willi. Harvard Dictionary of Music, 2nd ed. Cambridge, 1970.

Auer, Leopold. Violin Playing As I Teach It. New York, 1921.

Barbour, James Murray. "The Persistence of the Pythagorean Tuning System."
Scripta Mathematica, I, 4 (June 1933), 286-304.

_____. "Just Intonation Confuted." Music and Letters, XIX (January 1938), 48-60.

_____. "Irregular Systems of Temperament." (Paper read at the Thirteenth Annual Meeting of the American Musicological Society, Cambridge, December 29, 1947.)

_____. Tuning and Temperament. East Lansing, 1951.

Boyden, David D. "Prelleur, Geminiani and Just Intonation." Journal of the American Musicological Society, IV, 3 (Fall 1951), 202-219.

_____. The History of Violin Playing from Its Origins to 1761. London, 1965.

Cadek, Ottokar. "String Intonation in Theory and Practice." (Paper read at the M. T. N. A. -A. S. T. A. String Forum in Chicago, Illinois, January 1, 1949.) Published in Music Journal, VII, 3 (May-June 1949), 6-7 and 37-40.

Campagnoli, Bartolommeo. Metodo della meccanica progressiva per suonare il violino. Milan, no date. Also cataloged as Nouvelle méthode de la mechanique progressive du jeu de violon, Op.ᵃ 21. Milan, no date.

_____. Metodo per violino. Milan, 1797.

_____. A New Method for the Violin. London, no date.

Dounis, Demetrius C. The Absolute Independence of the Fingers in Violin Playing on a Scientific Basis, Op. 15. London, 1924-1926.

Ellis, Alexander J. "On the Calculation of Cents from Interval Ratios," p. 41[n] and

Appendix XX, Section C, pp. 446-451. In Hermann L. F. von Helmholtz's Sensations of Tone..., trans. by Alexander J. Ellis, 4th English edition. London, 1912. See also New York, 1954.

Flesch, Carl. The Art of Violin Playing, Book I. New York, 1924.

Greene, Paul C. "Violin Performance with Reference to Tempered, Natural and Pythagorean Intonation." University of Iowa Studies, Psychology of Music, IV (1937), 232-251.

Grove, Sir George. "Georg Andreas Sorge." Grove's Dictionary of Music and Musicians, edited by Eric Blom, 5th edition, VII, London, 1954, p. 972.

Guthrie, E. R., and H. Morrill. "Fusion of Non-Musical Intervals." American Journal of Psychology, XXXIX (1928).

Helmholtz, Hermann L. F. von. Sensations of Tone..., trans. by Alexander J. Ellis, 4th English edition. London, 1912.

Heman, Christine. Intonation auf Streichinstrumenten. Basel, 1964.

Hindemith, Paul. The Craft of Musical Composition, Book I. (Mainz, 1937); trans. by Arthur Mendel (London, 1942).

Lloyd, Llewelyn S. "Notes or Tones?--A Lost Opportunity." Monthly Musical Record, LXXVI, 881 (November 1946), 203-207.

_____. Intervals, Scales and Temperaments, edited by Hugh Boyle. London, 1963.

Nickerson, James F. "Intonation of Solo and Ensemble Performance of the Same Melody." The Journal of the Acoustical Society of America, XXI, 6 (November 1949), 593-595.

Ostrovsky, Fredy. Letter to the author, 1976.

Podnos, Theodor. "And Where Is Your 'A' Today?" Woodwind Magazine, I, 2 (December 1948), 3.

_____. "Woodwind Intonation." Woodwind Magazine, II, 4 (December 1949), 5 and 12.

_____. Bagpipes and Tunings. Detroit, 1974.

Pole, William. The Philosophy of Music, 6th ed. New York, 1924.

Poth, Adolphe. De ontwikkelingsgang der vioolmethodes tot omstreeks 1850. 's-Gravenhage, 1949.

Pratt, Waldo Selden, ed. "Georg Andreas Sorge." The New Encyclopedia of Music and Musicians, rev. ed. New York, 1929, p. 764.

Roberts, Chester. "Elements of Brass Intonation." The Instrumentalist (March 1975), 86-90.

Ross, Hugh. Letter to the author, 1967.

Sachs, Curt. The Rise of Music in the Ancient World, East and West. New York, 1943.

Scholes, Percy. "Pitch." The Oxford Companion to Music, 7th rev. ed. London, New York, and Toronto, 1947, pp. 731-735.

_____. "Temperament." The Oxford Companion to Music, 7th rev. ed. London, New York, and Toronto, 1947, pp. 923-928.

Shackford, Charles. "Some Aspects of Perception." Journal of Music Theory, Part I (November 1961), 162-202; Part II (April 1962), 66-90.

Shaw, George Bernard. "The Eternally New Problem of Pitch." Music in London 1890-94. London, 1932. Republished in Selmer Bandwagon, No. 77 (September 1975), 17-19.

Sorge, Georg Andreas. Vorgemach der musikalischen Komposition. 1745-1747.

Tartini, Giuseppe. Trattato di musica secondo la vera scienza dell' armonia. Padua, 1754.

Ware, John. Conversation with the author, 1980.

Young, Robert W. Table Relating Frequency to Cents. Elkhart, 1952.

ABOUT THE AUTHOR

Theodor Podnos was born in Boston, Massachusetts, where he studied with Richard Burgin, concertmaster of the Boston Symphony Orchestra. He has been concertmaster for Serge Koussevitzky at Tanglewood, Paul Whiteman in New York and for numerous radio presentations. As a trumpeter, he played on the staff of radio station WMGM for five years and for the American Broadcasting Company's "Omnibus" programs under Leonard Bernstein. Among twenty-five compositions to his credit, those which have received performances were scored for symphony orchestra, chamber groups and solo instruments. He has been a member of the Pro Musica String Quartet of Washington, D. C. and the Taliesen String Quartet on the Wisconsin estate of Frank Lloyd Wright. Two articles and a book, recently reprinted, comprise his past literary endeavors. He received his formal education at Peabody and Curtis Institutes and at Fairleigh Dickinson and Boston Universities.

In Europe and the United States, particularly at Columbia University, his lectures have concerned the history, construction and tunings of wind and string instruments. He is now a member of the first violin section of the New York Philharmonic.

190 / Intonation for Strings, Winds, and Singers

69, 74; passing notes marked with, 76. See also beginning pages of Chapters 6 to 9, and 13 to 16
Chordal Intonation: history of, 51-53; the system, 56-141 passim; passing notes tuned with, 76
Chords: the Dominant, in major or minor keys, 63-64; four-note, tunings of, 67, 89, 90, 113, 121-127, 129-134 passim, 136-141; augmented-sixth, in modulation and enharmonicism, 122-125 passim. See also Table of Contents
Clusters: semitone, 26, 30-32
Combination tones, 178 n1
Conductors: Zubin Mehta, 9; Hugh Ross, 44; double-stopped study for, 92; marking of scores by, 153; scores for, 154-165
Contemporary music. See Atonality
Contest: Interval System vs. Chordal Intonation, 76, 90

Desk work: marking arrows and chord symbols, 76
Difference tones. See Third tones
Dissonances: acceptable tuning, 58-59 passim, 69-71, 75
Dont, Jacob: Etude 3, reduced range for study of, 105
Double-stops, 92-99 passim; shifting to minor-3rd, 93; easy major-3rd, 93; études with, 96, 97, 98, 99, 104. See also Scales
Dounis, Demetrius C., 172
Duets: performance of, 9; for violins, 93-95, 98, 99, 103-104, 106-109; for winds or voice, 95, 97, 103-104; for winds, 106-109; atonal, 144-145

Electricity: similarity to Gravitation Theory, 31-32
Enharmonicism, 123; of Campagnoli, 11; in speed, 26; of Diminished-7th harmonies, 115-116; of augmented-6th chords, 123, 127 n3; in études, 133-134; difference between augmented 4th and diminished 5th, 142-143, 146 n2; in ensembles,

143-146 passim; use of equal temperament in, 144
Ensembles: double-stops in, 26, 28, 92; central notes in, 33; wind, 44; tunings in, 51; rehearsals of, 75; pretraining for, 100; a study for, 103-104; enharmonicism in, 143-146 passim; atonality in, 144-146; difficult quartet music for, 152-165
Equal temperament: history of, 8-9, 13 n3; measurements of, 46-47; a standard from which to deviate, 56; matching, in accompaniment, 69-70; imperfect 5th of, 73
Errors: chances of, 10, 51
Evolution of tunings, 8-9, 10, 61
Experiments: in different tempos, 19-20; with pentatonicism, 43; with Gravitation Theory, 43; university, 49-51 passim, 177 (See also Shackford); with Chordal Intonation, 51-53; with violin tunings, 59; with Tartini third tones, 176-177; for winds and singers, 179-180
Extension: to play minor 3rds, 93; whole-tone, 169. See also Fingers: stretching of

Feuermann, Emanuel: tunings of, 49
Fifth: flatted, chord, 121; augmented, chord, history of, 138 n1
Fifths. See Intervals
Fingerholes: sizes of, 43
Fingerings: awkward, 69, 142-143; strange, 172; for relaxation, 173
Fingers: pressed together, 15, 20-21, 30-32, 33-34, 37-39, 57-58, 67, 173-174; small, stretching of, 21, 93; small, in upper positions, 33-34; broad, 33; lifting up, 33, 83; stretching of 21, 67-68, 95, 99, 168-169, 170, 171-173; gauging of, 166-168; strengthening of 172, 175 n2
Five-note. See Pentatonic
Flesch, Carl, 51; semitones of, 33, 35 n2
Flutists: false tunings of, 44
Folk music: pentatonic, 42; neutral tunings in, 175
Forty intonations to the octave, 51
Fourths. See Intervals
Frequencies, 46, 174